Blood of the Earth

By

Maury Stoner

Contents

PROLOGUE

The Industrial Revolution seemed to be moving at the speed of light at the beginning of the 19th century as it began and spread across Europe and then on to a young, rapidly growing United States. Like the internet.com boom of the 1990s, over a hundred years earlier, a golden age of capitalism ushered in a tremendous surge of personal wealth in America. The massive wave in manufacturing across the country provided high-paying jobs, and along with it came an insatiable desire for the latest in technology, medicine, food, clothing, and transportation. Bringing these commodities to consumers as fast as possible was vital. Transportation had quickly evolved beyond horse-drawn wagons to major advances in railroads, ocean freighters, automobiles, and eventually airplanes. The need to create a faster supply chain to carry goods from farms and factories to the consumer was accomplished.

In the first decade of the 1900s, construction had begun on the Titanic, an enormous engineering feat not only for its day, but today it remains one of the largest passenger ships ever built at nearly 900 feet in length. The Wright brothers, who made their first successful flight of the Kittyhawk Flyer, and of course, Henry Ford's assembly line in Highland Park,

Michigan, began cranking out a Model T every 15 Minutes. An astonishing achievement in production efficiency that, to this day, is difficult to achieve.

All of these incredible advances have one significant thing in common—oil. Oil had become the lifeblood of the modern world, and the internal combustion engine was its heart. Oil field workers from Pennsylvania, California, Texas, Oklahoma, and several other states would soon have all the work they could handle. A blessing during a time when their livelihood of supplying kerosene for lanterns was being jeopardized by Thomas Edison's new electric light bulb.

While the technique of derrick-style oil drilling dates back to 347 AD in China, when hollow bamboo stalks were used, amazingly, the technology had only marginally advanced when the first commercial oil well went into operation in Poland in 1853.

Chapter 1

POP.…..POP.POP. Like most people, Dr. Fred Ressner had never heard the sound of a semi-automatic, 9-millimeter handgun before, at least not in real life. Rolling his ankle on the broken concrete sidewalk, he lost his battle with gravity and nearly fractured his wrist as he crashed hard to the ground. He narrowly dodged the three hollow-point bullets that whizzed by his head and punctured the bricks of the building behind him. As he was falling, Dr. Ressner heard the three popping sounds, immediately followed by the squeal of car tires, but the fall distracted his attention.

After testing his ankle and wrist, he casually sat up, brushed himself off, and looked around to see where the noise came from. Not seeing anything out of the ordinary, he simply shrugged it off to a group of students across the street he assumed were setting off firecrackers to celebrate the end of the school year. Besides, he thought only a maniac would be firing a gun that close to campus.

Between enjoying the incredible beauty of the scenic Colorado campus and struggling with anxiety over the presentation he was about to give to the top faculty members at the university, Dr. Ressner was nearly in a trance as he strolled toward campus. He was so deep in thought that he didn't even connect the noises to the large, intimidating black SUV with blacked-out windows as it sped away. He wouldn't realize it until much later, but Dr. Fred Ressner had just survived an assassination attempt.

In 1876, just five months before our 18th president, Ulysses S. Grant, officially named the bicentennial state of Colorado as the thirty-eighth state in the country, The University of Colorado in Boulder was founded. Soon after that day, by the middle of May each year, the postcard beauty of the Boulder campus would become full of contradictions. Crocus that bravely burst forth during a week of mild weather could be blanketed with snow the next week. The confidence on the smiling faces of the seniors who would soon be graduating, who for the last 9 months were at the top of the college food chain, would soon be bitch slapped away by the harsh reality of actually finding employment in the field they majored. Soon, most of them would nearly go into shock when they would receive their first payment due notice on mountains of student loan debt.

The relatively quiet calm before the storm, while students were cramming for finals, signaled to the faculty and staff that the summer session would soon be opening the flood gates of a fresh crop of eager and excited skulls full of hormones. The first day of classes was a warm one this year as Dr. Fred Ressner casually strolled by a few remaining piles of grey, slushy snow and mingled in with vibrant yellow daffodils as he fondly reminisced of his time here as a student.

Once he had chosen from one of a dozen or so job offers from refineries and oil exploration companies, Ressner went straight off to work after graduating from college. In a few short years, he would soon become a leading petroleum geologist and hydro physicist for two of the largest energy companies in the United States. During his long, distinguished career, he was credited with several major breakthrough innovations in oil, natural gas, and coal exploration. His most notable discoveries included an inexpensive process to extract methane gas trapped within coal shale, inventing a horizontal drilling technique, now known as fracking, and his revolutionary theories on crude oil migration through cracks in the earth's crust. Dr. Ressner's advances had directly resulted in hundreds of billions of dollars of added profits for his employers as new oil fields were expanded and tapped that were previously thought to be dry or were not even known to exist at all.

Having published 2 books, some 35 magazine articles, dozens of trade manuscripts, and being a high-level member of management teams at two energy companies meant that Dr. Fred could have lived just about anywhere in the world he wanted. However, returning to his childhood roots in central Colorado after retirement allowed him to remain involved in teaching the next generation of great scientists while also being able to enjoy his favorite pastime—fly fishing.

The university didn't have the earth sciences department; it came after his time as a student. If there were ever a poster child for the curriculum requirements to achieve a degree in this field, it would have been Fred Ressner. Having an incredibly ambitious college transcript that was top-loaded in advanced biology, chemistry, geology, hydro physics, and mechanical engineering didn't keep Fred off the Dean's list often. In addition to his unassuming intelligence, he also had a friendly, outgoing personality that was always supportive, never wasting an opportunity to help a classmate with an assignment. If there was a downside to having a genuine and likable personality, for Fred, it meant that it wasn't easy for him to stay on course and power through college while turning down countless invitations to frat parties and pregaming festivities. Growing up as an only child, his parents had instilled maturity and discipline in Fred at an early age that many of his college counterparts were yet to acquire. Dorm mates that acted like they had found the key to the candy store the day they arrived on campus would often hassle him, saying while he's at it, he might also get a degree for being the most boring student on campus. The joke would soon be on them as his impressive drive and dedication to academics paid off big time when he entered the field of petroleum engineering immediately after graduating and began making serious bank.

The only time Fred wasn't studying was when he was hanging out with Kim. They had met the first semester of their sophomore year in the campus cafeteria and would soon be spending about any free time they had together. Attending college mainly because her parents insisted but also being pressured by a few of her high school friends, Kim was reluctant but finally committed to four more years of school. Although she wasn't exactly crazy about higher academia, she was no slacker either; plus, having a mild case of OCD had also worked to her advantage as she was able to excel in her classes and earn a BA in marketing.

After marrying Fred, her college sweetheart, Kim wanted to stay home to raise their two children. Once both children were in high school, she was finally able to put her degree to work. So, she launched a successful home decorating business that catered to her wealthy clients who lived between Denver and Boulder.

After college and a few decades of demanding work, Fred's professional career had finally run its course. He was able to walk away with all the money he needed to retire in comfort at an age young enough that allowed him to pursue the next phase of his life that he had been secretly planning for several years. Reaching out to his alma mater to inquire about a faculty position, Fred was immediately offered several honorary positions, but he wasn't interested in any hyped-up, meaningless figurehead titles. Preferring to be more involved and hands-on, he requested that he be hired as a professor of the first-class dedicated to renewable energy resources—a class that wasn't even offered at the time.

Hobbling on his wounded ankle and favoring his achy wrist, Fred finally made his way to the faculty lounge. Once his nerves settled, he was able to outline the curriculum to the university president and several deans. Fred received some minor resistance to his concept, but one dean, in particular, was adamantly opposed. Fred's idea for the class was a unique and controversial concept, unlike any other renewable energy classes the faculty had ever heard of at other universities. Ultimately, the deans and president caved in and agreed to Fred's terms mainly due to their recently enacted program to attract more prestigious faculty members. They felt that having Dr. Fred on staff would help in their efforts to build a higher caliber staff. Not only did Fred persuade the university to establish an entirely new program for him, but he was also provided with his own lab to conduct his ongoing experiments. He was also given the interns of his choice to assist with his continuing research.

Having never taught before, Fred was fairly intimidated on his first day of class when he pushed open the wooden double door, walked into the auditorium, and saw nearly 80 students staring back at him. He hadn't felt the rapid heartbeat, shaky knees, and clammy, sweaty palms since he was in the hospital to witness the birth of his first child some 25 years earlier, but even then, Fred had passed out just before the delivery.

"Wow, are you kids lost, or am I? This is renewable energy 101, correct?"

Drawing some laughs from the class, it didn't take long for Fred to break the ice. Some of the students already felt that Fred could be one of their favorite teachers with his easy, laid-back style. He received the warm reception he hoped for and could only think that having no clue as to what the hell he was doing was actually going to work to his advantage. Beginner's luck, he humbly thought, never one to give himself the credit he deserved.

"Welcome, everyone. Today, we are about to undertake a new adventure together, so hang on tight; it should be a bumpy but fun ride. Since this is our first day together, I thought I would start off nice and easy by simply telling you the story of a different type of renewable energy. You may have heard of it. Black gold? Texas tea?"

The class stared back with faces as blank as the massive chalkboard behind him.

"Crude oil!"

"Wait, what the hell? Seriously dude? No F'ing way?"

It was immediately obvious to Fred that most of his students had been indoctrinated into the world of manufactured climate change. They were clearly disappointed, if not downright upset, that they had just spent their parents' money or gone further into debt to listen to what they believed to be total nonsense.

They felt they were about to be gaslighted. The warm, fuzzy feelings of just a few moments earlier were quickly replaced with confusion and disappointment. Fred expected that he would be getting a strong reaction from his class, but he was in no way prepared for the abuse of freedom of speech that had suddenly begun raining down on him, and he desperately tried to salvage the train wreck unraveling in front of him.

"I know, I know. You were all probably expecting to hear about wind power, right? Those hideous, massive blades and turbines are so loud that they scare off birds and other wildlife permanently away from their natural habitats. Moreover, according to the Saint Francis Arboreal and Wildlife Association, just in the United States alone, between 13 million and 39 million birds are killed every year by the spinning blades. During high winds, they can reach speeds up to 200 miles per hour—speeds so fast that the blades aren't even visible to the birds causing them to fly directly to their death.

Some of you may have heard of the Altamont Pass located in California, the country's largest migratory route of Golden Eagles. Although these birds are protected by federal law, for some reason, the Obama administration signed a 30-year permit that allowed the construction of a massive windmill farm that kills an estimated 115 to 120 Golden Eagles every year. And not to mention, trying to live anywhere near them can be nearly impossible due to the constant, mind-numbing hum.

A study done at a windmill farm located in Northern Indiana proved that insects were being affected not only by the noise but also possibly by magnetic fields created by the turbines that confuse them; as a result, the crops in the area weren't being pollinated. Imagine a massive field of giant windmills producing about 40 decibels of noise so that when you put 20, 30, or more together, you may as well be sitting front row at a Black Sabbath concert."

"Ha-ha, what is a Black Sabbath, Dr. Ressner?" one student asked.

Realizing he had just dated himself about as old as the oil he was there to teach about, Fred replied, "I meant the Foo Fighters. Now, keep in mind that since windmills only function and produce power on average about 30% of the time depending on wind conditions, the rest of the time, they just sit there looking ridiculous."

Then there is also an enormous environmental impact of building, transporting, and installing giant windmills. This is a massive undertaking that requires numerous factories that, by the way, are powered mainly by coal, oil, or natural gas. Then they are loaded and delivered across the country on giant 18-wheelers that burn tons of diesel fuel in the process, and they finally are installed. A mind-boggling 600 cubic meters of concrete is required for each windmill to ensure they don't get blown over by high winds. That's 1500 tons of concrete per windmill, guys! When you factor all these things in, along with the labor costs required to maintain a single windmill, you are looking at an ROI, the return on investment, at somewhere around 40 years to recoup. The problem is the average life expectancy of one of these monsters is only about 20 years. If there are any math majors here who can please explain to me how that adds up, I'd like to talk after class!"

Everyone, windmills are a 16th-century technology that has been modified, advertised, and monetized through either bribery by powerful lobbyists or pressure from the media. They have been repackaged and sold to Washington politicians as a silver bullet. The problem is the bullets are blanks!"

Or some of you might like to talk about electric cars, the latest rage, right? Elon Musk, Tesla, yada yada yada... You plug them in, and voila, no gas, you just go. Clean, renewable transportation, right? But did you know that it takes about 500,000 gallons of water, another of our precious resources, to produce just 1 ton of lithium used for electric vehicle battery packs? Not to mention that toxic chemicals like hydrochloric acid are used in the mining process. Many of the lithium mines are located in poorer countries like those in the so-called lithium triangle countries of Chile, Bolivia, and Argentina. There are no strict environmental laws like we have in place in the United States to protect the workers or the environment. The result is that once these hazardous chemicals are depleted, they are typically just left behind or dumped. And who wants to talk about the child workers as young as seven years old that are basically forced to work for pennies while risking their lives every day? They are often exposed not only to tunnel collapses but also to the mining dust that can cause permanent damage to their young, still developing lungs. Not exactly environmentally friendly, huh?"

And lastly, we need to keep in mind that when you plug that "clean" EV in to recharge the battery that, currently, nearly 60% of the power generated in the entire world is still produced from burning coal, oil, or natural gas. Yes, people, you could possibly be driving a coal-powered car. If the current sales trends continue, even more fossil fuels will be needed not just to fuel the factories where they are built but also to meet the demand for electricity to keep your electric vehicles on the road."

Kids, what I am trying to point out is that there are two sides to every coin. If you choose to be a member of the woke, you need to know exactly what it is that you're waking up next to! So please, just bear with me for what's left of my 55 minutes while I share my story with you, and next week we all can debate it."

Once things calmed down, Fred proceeded, saying, "OK, let me just tell you all a story of a man they called Dry Hole Pete."

The name Dry Hole Pete drew a few more laughs from the class as they had finally settled down.

"OK, I hear you. Dry Hole Pete! It's a funny nickname but just stay with me. I think you will really like Dry Hole Pete and his story, and trust me, after my next lecture on Monday, this will all make a lot of sense to you. Here we go...."

University Colorado circa 1876

Chapter 2

"Nearly deaf from working side by side with monstrous oil derrick machinery for half of his life, 'Dry Hole' Pete had a gruff yet somehow effective way of communicating with his crew.

'Gimme another double-length pipe NOW, g'dammit,' he screeched.

This was no place for manners or patience. Pete had seen more than his share of horrific accidents during his career. Working conditions in the days before OSHA safety regulations routinely saw men crushed, maimed, and killed by split-second moments of indecision.

Tattered, thin, uneducated, and at just 36 years old, Pete was already too old for the brutally physical work his job demanded. However, Pete was respected by his crew—not so much for his keen ability to strike oil but for his ability to keep his crew as safe as possible under impossible conditions. Oil derrick work was beyond dirty. The grease and grime had become permanent stains on his body, just like the hideous, cartoonishly large-breasted mermaid tattoo he had gouged onto his forearm during a drunken weekend binge in Paris during World War 1. The stench of oil permeated his body, and the odor seemed to ooze out when he sweated.

The relentless clanging, grinding, and violent friction of steel on steel on an oil platform was overwhelming for most men who tried it. Combined with the mind-numbing vibration and tremendous noise of huge diesel engines, typically just feet away used to evacuate rock and muddy water from the borehole, this line of work was downright unbearable for most who attempted to earn a living as an oil rigger. In fact, most of Pete's crew had either gone or were on their way to going completely deaf. After years of working together in noisy silence with their ears plugged with whatever was available, riggers often communicated more by hand gestures and lip-reading than by hearing and shouting.

Determined and needing to somehow motivate a crew being punished by the blazing Southern California sun, Pete randomly barked out, "Let's make this damn hole bleed, boys!" He reloaded another wad of Beechnut between his remaining brown and black stained teeth, which he called his summer teeth—some 'r there, some 'r summer not. At the same time, he helped to set the double-length pipe into the kelly spinner. Pete could feel the end of his career creeping up his aching feet, legs, and back. Known as a wildcatter, Pete placed as much faith in hunches as he did in science.

The result of which was an unfortunate streak of recent dry wells that had led his boss to place Pete in charge of yet another long-shot well named the Skyview.

The original owner of the Skyview Well was a charismatic local grocery store owner named Ben Jewel. After years of growing boredom and complacency pawning produce, Mr. Jewel decided to venture into oil prospecting while reading one after another newspaper headlines about the latest big oil strike across the country. Beginning in Pennsylvania, then continuing to Ohio, Oklahoma, and Texas, the oil rush was on. The massive strike at the Spindle Top site in Beaumont, Texas, had inspired thousands of men across the country to leave their homes in search of the "black gold." But unlike those successes, an overconfident yet under-funded Mr. Jewel ran out of money after drilling 1,600 feet deep into the earth. Not surprising to anyone at the time, considering that the location of Mr. Jewel's rig was naively chosen based on his unfounded belief. Mr. Jewel believed that a random patch of red grass growing on a vacant lot on the far southwest side of town surely indicated that oil was lurking underneath. With most of his life savings now lying at the bottom of an empty hole, Jewel finally conceded and made the difficult decision to wash the lack of oil off his hands for good.

After returning to the comfortable familiarity of his grocery store, one day, Jewel received an offer to purchase the land and equipment from an unknown wildcatter named Pete. Although far from a generous offer, Jewel gladly accepted the buyout and hoped to put the whole ordeal behind him forever and move on. With new ownership now in place, drilling resumed. Forging into the earth 60 feet at a time by attaching two 30-foot sections of fitted pipe together, the workers called a double, Pete and his crew had reached a depth of 2,200 feet when a sudden, terrifying yet exhilarating feeling punched him right in the gut. If Pete had not sensed this experience before, he would have simply chalked it up to paranoia, exhaustion, or the bad stew he had for lunch. Trusting in his instincts and years of experience, Pete knew exactly the chaotic scene that was about to occur even though his younger, less experienced crew never had in all their years working in oil. The sudden sick sensation, like when you see a horrible accident, made Pete nauseous up until the adrenalin hit. The rush of energy now flowing through his veins gave the battered man the strength needed to overcome his fear and lead his crew. His worn-out body was instantly rejuvenated as Pete realized this was the very moment he had devoted most of his short life working in oil fields to experience.

Like a thousand freight trains rumbling beneath him, Pete's feet began to tickle from the intense vibration pulsating from nearly a half-mile below. Although he had enjoyed marginally successful oil strikes, Pete had only heard stories of what happens when a major well is hit. He instinctively knew that he and his crew were standing directly atop an enormous gusher, a well under immense pressure—enough pressure to blow the entire rig apart.

Pete's boss, the new owner of the Skyview site, had his own doubts about the prospect of the well. So, the under-sized diverters and capping equipment the company sent Pete was all they could use to cap the flow. Now that the crew had hit a high-pressure well, they had no way to contain the massive surge of oil. In a matter of seconds, the tremendous pressure violently and relentlessly pushed the crude up toward the surface like a geyser. 1,800 feet, 1,200 feet, 600 feet, and moving fast, the roaring sounded like a pissed-off tiger looking for an escape route, and Pete and his crew were standing directly over the beast's only exit. Sand and dirt danced around their feet while the rancid stench of crude oil produced in the belly of the earth millions of years ago violently blew out dozens of 5-inch, solid iron bore pipes like they were toothpicks.

Pete and his crew stumbled like the drunken sailors they were as they desperately fled the wooden platform before it exploded beneath them. At a pressure of over 20,000 pounds per square inch and over 20 feet in diameter, the immense gusher effortlessly launched thousands of pounds of piping, pumps, and engines hundreds of feet into the air as the crew ran for their lives. A thunderous explosion threw Pete and his crew to the ground as the crude finally reached the borehole.

'It's like we're back in the Navy, boys!' Pete shouted with the nervous excitement of a boy on Christmas morning.

Once reaching a safe distance, Pete forced himself to stand on his wiry legs and turn to witness what he had done. Overcome with emotion, his crew celebrated while they danced in the thick, oily waterfall. Incredibly, the Skyview remained an uncapped geyser for the next 18 months as it lost millions of gallons of crude and wreaked havoc on the surrounding area. Uncontrollably heaving and spewing a fine mist of the heavy, black syrup high into the sky, the grime was carried by the wind for miles and coated everything in its path. A thick, sticky film painted homes, buildings, and streets until the entire area resembled a glossy black and white photograph. People scrambled to evacuate their homes and businesses.

In the months following the strike, most of the trees and vegetation died, as did many pets and livestock animals. Spontaneous fires broke out in adjacent neighborhoods as inadvertent sparks from candles, gas lanterns, and machinery brought the black monster from the deep back to life.

Skyview continued to heave out over 90,000 barrels of oil every day until it finally began to taper down after 18 long months. Once it had tapered down to a manageable flow, the well was finally capped. However, by that time, the damage was already beyond anyone's wildest imagination. After a year and a half of uncontrolled flow of oil, the well bled out a mind-boggling 9.4 million barrels of oil, less than half of which was saved by diking and pumping it off into large holding tanks. There was so much oil collected in the hastily made dams that people, usually drunk men, would actually raft on it. However, enough oil was collected and sold from Skyview that the price of crude in the United States dropped by 50%.

To this day, Skyview is still the single largest oil spill disaster on American soil in the history of our country. As a matter of fact, more than 2½ times more oil was lost at Skyview than was at the second-largest oil spill in American history, i.e., the Deepwater Horizon accident that occurred off the coast of Louisiana in 2010, some 90 years after Skyview."

Finally done with his story, Fred and the students didn't notice that he had gone well over his allotted 55 minutes. When he was finally done with the lecture and the students began grabbing their backpacks and stood up to leave, a few of them gave Fred scattered, subdued applause as they filed out of the room. On the way out, one young lady turned to Fred and said, "Not really sure what that had to do with oil as a renewable energy, Dr. Ressner, but that was a pretty cool story."

While most of them still didn't believe or want to hear that oil is renewable energy and is as abundant as water, Fred felt that as long as they at least liked their teacher, it would make his job of reprogramming them much easier.

Skyview Gusher

Chapter 3

Dr. Fred was getting annoyed. His hand-made flies kept getting snagged on the limbs and the large, smooth rocks at the bottom of the small river. The river had been made even more shallow due to a well below average snow melts in the Rocky Mountains. Fred didn't really seem to care that the water was a little too shallow for fly fishing today. Standing in the cool, crystal-clear water had become a type of therapy for him over the years.

As far as hobbies go, he wasn't crazy about exercising. Not only was he lousy at golf, he thought it was about as exciting as flossing his teeth. So, whenever he would have free time, Fred would come down to the serene peace of the valley to fish, smoke a cigar, occasionally have some bourbon from the flask he would put in the cool water, and think.

He was doing just that when he was suddenly startled as he heard the excitement in a young man's shaky voice coming out of nowhere shouting, "Dr. Fred, we've got another one."

Fred knew that his day of fishing was over for good. With large black bodies and white feathers on their wings,

Lark Buntings, the state bird of Colorado, had quietly surrounded Fred and had been keeping a close watch on him
and their nests. Also startled by the yelling, the flock bolted
from the safety of their hiding spots in bushes to high up
in the Aspens as the news flash boomed across the valley,
gently flowing stream while the ensuing echo sounded as if
someone was mocking him.

"Dr. Fred? Dr. Fred?"

"Jason, what's with all the hubbub, bub? I heard you
the first 3 times."

"Fred, we just found another source of clean oil!"
"That is fantastic news. Now, let's give the greenback
trout a moment; they no longer seem interested in my bait."

"Oh dude, I'm totally sorry, man."

Far too slender to appear to be healthy and sporting a
shaggy, splotchy patch of facial hair and dreadlocks, Jason
was one of the three interns Dr. Fred had chosen to work on
his petroleum research team at the University.

At just twenty-one years old, Jason was usually a laid-
back, tie-dye tee-shirt-wearing, modern-day hippie, still

common in the area. Although he had recently turned old enough to drink, Jason preferred other, more natural plants and herbs for relaxation rather than alcohol. Still, when something excited him, which wasn't very often, it could be quite a show. A nervous habit, his vocal cords would squeeze tight, causing his normally deep voice to go up by a couple of octaves until he would actually sound as if he were kicked hard directly in the cojones. If that weren't enough, growing up in Brooklyn made the use of his hands to communicate second nature, but Jason could take it to a whole new level. His animated body language came into play as total use of arms, hands, eyes, and whatever parts he couldn't control would join in the conversation; if you didn't know better, you might think he was on the verge of a mild seizure.

Jason was a good kid, though, and Dr. Fred saw the many qualities in him that most others couldn't, only because of his sloppy, outward appearance. His overall look and attitude resulted in several opportunities with jobs and girls to pass him by ever since his teenage years. If there was one thing that Jason did have a hard time expressing, it was telling Dr. Fred how grateful he was for being able to see past his soft exterior and giving him a chance on his team of interns. He considered Dr. Fred a sort of his father figure, but he could never admit to something like that for fear of risking his carefree, whatever, man persona. Deep down, though, Jason was a kind, considerate, and respectful modern-day hippie. Not at all the rebellious, intitled type that some people assumed he was based simply on his appearance.

"Jason, are you certain it's not another case of false-positive test results? The last two reports of empty oil well replenishment I've received turned out to be false alarms."

"Oh, fer sure, man, we're posifreakingtively sure on this one, doc! We were able to score the disclosure documents from the defunct Standard Oil Company. This site was locked down and abandoned in 1912 after it was confirmed to have been pumped out drier than a hemp biscuit. And doc, the kicker is that since there is an absence of biomarkers, it means the new oil is totally unique, and it's migrating from underground and not from another field."

"Excellent work, Jason! Let me pack up my gear. Why don't you round up the rest of the team and meet me in my office in about an hour? We'll all check it out together."

Dr. Fred could have easily made it back to his office in under 30 minutes if not for the meticulous re-packing job he was about to undertake. He took considerable pride in his hand-sewn Prince Nymph flies and vintage Orvis Centrepin rod and reel combo that had caught enough greenback trout to feed a small country. Fred always ensured his equipment was well-protected as he securely packed and stored it away on the back seat. He then climbed up into the plush, velvety leather seat, closed the tight-fitting door that completely blocked any outside noise, and entered into the complete silence and luxury of the cab—his beautiful brand-new Ford F-250 Lariat pickup truck. Fred loved his truck and felt the combination of ruggedness, power, and comfort fit his lifestyle perfectly. Though he was known to be a real bookworm in college, he also had a reputation as a headbanger in his youth, but today he was in the mood for something different.

It was a gloriously crisp, sunny day without a cloud in the deep blue skies above central Colorado. To further enhance his mood, Fred chose to crank up Beethoven's Ode to Joy until 1000 watts of pure bliss were pumping out of the 10 speakers. He was conducting with one hand and steering with the other as he navigated his way up then back down the narrow mountain pass toward his lab on campus.

It took him a while, but he finally realized that his grip on the steering wheel was so tight that his knuckles had turned white, and his fingers had nearly gone numb. Not because of the blaring music or the steep winding road, but because he knew that if Jason's news was confirmed to be right, it would be the second verified account of a major oil field replenishment in the last 24 months.

Besides fly fishing and being close to his childhood home, another contributing factor in his decision to return to middle Colorado and become a semi-recluse was the dubious reputation he had earned several years earlier.

After sharing his belief in one of the most groundbreaking yet controversial theories on the history of oil creation with his colleagues, his career path went into a swift downward spiral; for the most part, he had become an outcast among his peers. Could this really be the moment that had consumed Dr. Fred for so many years? Could this possibly be the vindication he had been searching for that would lead to his return to prominence and the glorious resurrection of his once bright and shiny reputation?

He had amassed all the material possessions he wanted, including his truck, and many others he didn't need. He was proud of the fruits of his hard work, the years of extensive continuing education, travels around the world, numerous publications, and the high-profile jobs and huge salaries that came with them. At this point in his life, however, what he wanted most of all, what he needed and craved more than anything, was to finish what he had started. He somehow had to find the proof he needed to once and for all end the debate and prove that the abiogenesis theory of oil creation is real and present it to the entire world. Fred felt that finally being able to flip his colleagues a big double bird and say I told you so would somehow make everything in his life right again.

Chapter 4

Dr. Ressner considered himself a mentor to the 3 interns who greeted him like nerdy groupies at his subterranean lab at the center of campus. It was a prime location, and the university was happy to provide it to an esteemed scientist like Dr. Fred despite his recent questionable reputation. In fact, Dr. Fred was himself trying desperately to shed that dubious reputation.

"Good afternoon, Dr. Fred. How many fish you catch?" Unlike most Japanese who craved and often consumed the best sushi in the world, his intern, Sangen, loathed any kind of fish, raw or cooked, and wanted nothing to do with it. Her parents had named her in honor of the goddess of fire enshrined at the summit of Mt. Fuji in Japan. Sangen's father wasn't happy with the idea of her being so far from home, but he reluctantly chose for her to attend college in Colorado due to its similarities to the much smaller Japanese Alps. Sangen's father felt the beauty of the natural scenery might help her not to become so homesick. A human spark plug, at an even five feet and one hundred pounds, her positive energy and playful enthusiasm were invigorating to the middle-aged Dr. Fred. Like his two other interns, Jason and Henry, Sangen was also recruited because of her double majors in chemistry and biology. However, unlike Jason and Henry, she was also a staunch environmentalist. Fred thought that if he could convince Sangen that the theory of abiogenic oil was real, he could convince anyone.

"Not my day for trout, Sangen. Hopefully, we'll have better luck fishing for oil. Where is the new strike located?" Dr. Fred asked while firing up his laptop.

"Oh, check it out, doc; this place is located about five miles outside of some little podunk town called Titusville, Pennsylvania," Replied Jason.

"Now that's interesting! Little old Titusville. Located in Northwest Pennsylvania, founded in the 1790s, it's considered to be the birthplace of the modern oil industry in America," said Dr. Fred.

"Wait. What!"

Henry, Dr. Fred's third intern, was surprised to hear this as he pushed his thick black glasses back up his large, oily nose. Though he was a brilliant student, Henry could be described by some as a Sheldon. A nerd who, even though was now in his 20s, would rather spend time playing online video games and chatting with virtual people than spending quality time with real ones.

Growing up in far northwest Pennsylvania near Titusville, Henry's parents would often encourage him to get outside and play in the fresh air. They even tried getting him involved in youth sports leagues, but Henry only wanted to self-shelter and keep himself company. This upbringing resulted in an award childhood that eventually led to a brief Marilyn Manson phase when he entered his late teenage years. Henry became quite a loner. His only social interaction was with a small pack of like-minded kids, who would always sit in the school cafeteria to protect themselves from being hassled by other kids.

The only trouble he had ever been in was during his senior year. Henry hacked into the school's server and modified the profile information of a few teachers he didn't like. To make matters worse, he then proceeded to replace their pictures with ones he had lifted from a porn site. A self-taught computer expert, Henry, wrote his first code for a gaming app when he was only 14. Unfortunately, his distorted sense of humor backfired after the school's IT Department traced the nude pictures back to his IP address. Henry was brilliant but careless—a trait that would stay with him for the rest of his life. His parents begged the school district not to expel him and after the prank that earned him a one-week suspension, he never showed any other signs that would alert his parents or teachers that he was any kind of threat. He enjoyed the brief, misguided respect he got from the prank from some other kids who were also on the fringe of society.

Henry continued his 4-year run and remained in high honors every semester of high school while taking dozens of advanced placement classes. Looking past the piercings, black fingernails, and the spiked dog chain around his neck, his parents always loved him. Eventually, they accepted and understood that Henry was simply different from other kids.

Having grown up like an introvert on steroids, he had only a basic knowledge of the history of the town he came from. When the internship opportunity came up, Henry was introduced to Dr. Fred by a dean on staff; ironically, it was the same dean who had strongly opposed the class and the hiring of Fred. For some reason, after all of his initial resistance to Ressner and his course syllabus, he approached Fred and asked, "Dr. Ressner, do me a solid and give the kid a shot. It might just be good for your career."

The dean introduced Henry to Fred, then as abruptly as he had barged into the lab, he left without bothering to stay and talk or at least say thanks. As the dean turned to leave the lab, he pulled his cell phone out of his jacket pocket and headed down a back hallway that happened to have remarkable acoustics that allowed Fred to hear every word of the dean's conversation, including the last four words, i.e., "He's in; it's done."

Fred had no idea who or what the dean was talking about; he assumed that he was just sharing the good news with Henry's parents. Since that day, something in Fred's sub-conscience just prevented him from being fond of Henry despite the fact he reminded Fred of himself during his head-banging phase back in high school. Fred thought to himself the friction he felt toward Henry was probably due to the fact that he was more or less threatened by a colleague to add him to his team of interns.

"Why is Titusville so interesting, Dr. Fred?"

"Well, Henry, first off, records show that as far back as the 1400s, the Seneca Indians of Pennsylvania would use a thick, black tar substance to repair small leaks in their canoes and teepees. Then hundreds of years later, the locals that settled in the area would use the oily tar to lubricate the wheels on their wagons. In fact, the tar was so abundant in Western Pennsylvania that it had become a major nuisance and was threatening the growing business of salt mining in the area; remember, salt brine is often found in areas where there is an abundance of oil. The thick, black goo would literally ooze right up from the ground and up to the surface, as well as flow into creeks and down into the mining caverns. This caused a major problem extracting the salt, which in turn jeopardized the entire industry."

Around 1845, a 30-year-old man named Samuel Kier, who owned and operated a salt company about 100 miles south of Titusville in Pittsburg, was becoming increasingly concerned as the tar had significantly reduced his salt production. Knowing that the tar could burn, Kier saw potential in the sticky goo and thought he might be able to make lemonade out of lemons, or in this case, the tar. After months of countless trial and error, he finally came up with a successful method to distill and refine the tar and turn it into a profitable product—kerosene. Kier began selling the new product as fuel for lamps, now giving consumers an option to the whale blubber that was commonly used at the time."

Unlike the fishy smell of burning whale blubber oil, the high-quality kerosene Kier sold contained a very low amount of sulfur, producing little odor or fumes when burned. Soon, his lamp fuel business was booming. Keir needed to increase production. Since his equipment could only refine enough tar to produce about 5 gallons of kerosene at a time, he was severely limited in production capacity. Desperately wanting to expand his growing business, he thought that if he could only dig or drill deeper into the earth, he could extract the oil right from the ground before the oil had a chance to dry and become the thick, messy tar. Also, it would make the distillation process much faster. Since Kier had no knowledge of drilling, he recruited a man named Edwin Drake from the Rock Oil Company in Titusville, where news of Kier's lamp fuel had quickly spread."

While most people thought the idea of drilling for oil was just short of crazy, Kier remained unphased by his critics and committed to his dream and likewise, had convinced Drake to remain persistent right along with him. Mainly by providing him with a generous weekly paycheck. Eventually, the two men had finally succeeded in their work as they had managed to drill down deep enough to discover the thinner viscosity oil that would be much easier for Kier to distill. After their humble beginning, Kier eventually established himself as the father of oil refining in the United States, while Drake is still considered today as the father of modern oil drilling in America."

Once Drake's work was done and he finished teaching Kier how to drill, he returned to Titusville, where the same phenomenon of seeping oil that Kier had experienced was occurring. Although the Rock Oil Company was now defunct, Drake, who had only a little money remaining from his job working for Kier, was able to convince a local bank to give him a loan. One that the banker nearly lost his job over.

He took the $200 loan and used it to purchase the equipment he needed to drill for his own oil."

Using a tiny, underpowered 6-horsepower steam engine, he was only able to drill down a few feet a day. Not only was the drill too slow, but often the hole he had dug the day before would collapse on itself overnight, creating a frustrating and time-wasting two steps forward, one step back situation. Not short on ingenuity, Drake thought that if he could simply insert an iron pipe down into the borehole and place the auger inside the pipe, the hole might remain open when the drill was shut off for the day. The idea worked. Using this technique, Drake and his small crew were able to drill down to just shy of 70 feet when they did it. They had found the thin, lightweight crude that was so abundant in Titusville that it could hardly contain itself underground."

Soon after the success of his first well, Drake founded the Seneca Oil Company and was one of the first to establish drilling operations in Titusville. Unfortunately, word of the success of his closed borehole invention had made it out, and many others who had learned of the oil had begun to flock to Titusville and copied Drake's idea. Regrettably, for Drake, he did not have the foresight to patent his simple invention. His technique was copied and was being used by virtually every rig in Titusville. As a result of his oversight, Drake was soon overrun by dozens of larger companies with much deeper pockets. Sadly, he was left nearly penniless despite his significant contribution to the industry." *But hell, at least he still had a good reputation,* Fred grudgingly thought to himself.

"Anyway, back to the point. The farmers in Titusville had first noticed the oil seeping right up from the ground and into their creeks and fields."

"For real, Dr. Fred, you mean like Jed and the Beverly Hillbillies?" Henry joked.

"Actually, Henry, yes, exactly like the Beverly Hillbillies. Soon after the discovery of oil in Titusville, the podunk, as Jason called it, quickly became flooded with every imaginable type of capitalist, or opportunist, depending on your point of view. Prospectors, lawyers, bankers, and thousands of laborers made their way to the sleepy village of around 250 people causing it to explode to over 10,000 in only a matter of months."

Like the California gold rush in the late 1840s, the Pennsylvania oil rush was now full speed ahead, and everyone wanted a piece of it. Of course, along with the near-instantaneous surge of prosperity in the area, there also came many bottom feeders like pickpockets, bootleggers, and prostitutes looking to profit in less conventional or legal ways.

As Titusville would soon be known as the first oil boomtown in America, the once beautiful, pristine country-side of rolling wooded hills had quickly become littered by a forest of massive oil derricks that resembled huge, creepy, wooden insects. They were given names by their owners like the Vampire, the Scared Cat, Sleeping Beauty, and dozens of others.

Seeing the massive explosion in oil production happening in Titusville and realizing that the growing crude oil business would soon lead to the decline of whaling, reporters hired by whaling operations were sent from large city newspapers, particularly from the East Coast. They wrote that 'the oilmen were now harpooning Mother Earth herself instead of the whales' as they tried in vain to stop the inevitable transition to oil."

Incredibly, within a year, there were more millionaires per capita living in tiny Titusville, Pennsylvania, than in any other city in the world! Men such as JD Rockefeller of Standard Oil made incredible fortunes from the Titusville oil. In just a few short years, the Standard Oil Company had become the leader and grown so large that it was considered to be a monopoly by the United States government. In fact, Standard became so big that the government would eventually forcibly divide the company up into Exxon, Chevron, Mobile, and nearly 30 other smaller oil companies.

At just 31 years old, Rockefeller had become the world's first billionaire. Once, he had leveraged his great fortune from oil into pipelines, railroads, plastics, and then on to his most profitable business yet of pharmaceutical manufacturing. Rockefeller's estimated net worth, adjusted for today's inflation and currency rate, would be somewhere well over $700 billion. Nobody really knows exactly how much money he had due to some creative bookkeeping by teams of high-priced tax attorneys."

"No way, man, that's more than Elon Musk, Warren Buffet, and Jeff Bezos combined!"

"That's actually right, Jason. Now, imagine the power that comes with that kind of wealth, generational wealth, which meant his children's, children's, children would never have to worry about money."

Anyway, after the Titusville wells were eventually pumped dry, Rockefeller and the others had long moved on. Less than 20 years after it all began, little Titusville, Pennsylvania, went from a hustling boom town to a bust town. Hundreds of broken-down oil derricks were simply deserted and left behind to rot. The massive structures that the oil companies left behind were not only an eyesore, but they were also quite unsafe as young boys were often hurt playing and climbing the massive wooden towers. Outsiders said the derricks resembled skeletons of prehistoric monsters, but to the locals and those that choose to stay in Titusville, the derricks were reminders of better times."

"Like empty beer bottles the morning after an off-campus party!" chimed Henry.

"Yeah, like you have ever been to a party, Henry, hahaha!" Sangen teased.

Dr. Fred had become intimately familiar with the area during his years scouting oil for the Shale Energy Company. Since that time, significant advances in horizontal and diagonal drilling technology have provided access to oil reserves previously considered out of reach. However, the reason the newly discovered Titusville oil was so important to Dr. Fred was that laboratory analysis had shown that the oil had migrated from within a layer of rock located well below the Mississippian period, closer to the Devonian period.

"But Dr. Fred, rock formations from the Devonian period were formed between 320 and 415 million years ago. Dinosaurs weren't even around until millions of years later in the Cretaceous and Triassic periods."

"That's correct, Henry. Dinosaurs didn't arrive on the scene until about 230 million years ago and died out around 65 million years ago.

Also, as we know that oil is lighter than water and naturally floats, there is no way possible, even with migration, for it to have simply sunk to that tremendous depth. We are talking miles deep, deeper than any true vertical oil drill has ever been."

"Dr. Fred, what lab testing are you talking about, and how can you be so sure that this oil is coming from that far below the earth's crust?"

"Jason, do you remember first-year biology?"

"How could I forget it? Heather Hunt was in that class. A total hottie!"

"Alrighty, then. I am so glad the class made such an impression on you, Jason. So, to refresh your memory, samples taken of the recent oil discovery in Titusville show an absence of oleanane."

Jason's eyes opened wide. "Oh, Cool, now I remember. Oleanane is the residual organic compound left behind from flowering angiosperms, the kind of plants you can't smoke...."

"A-Plus Jason. It doesn't make up for that Heather Hunt crack, but good."

Developed by Stanford University, oleanane sampling has been a widely accepted and used tool in the oil industry to determine the age of oil. This technique is used in conjunction with infrared, ultrasonic, and, on more rare occasions, helium detection to classify the age and depth of crude oil. By determining the approximate age and the depth, companies can then decide whether or not the cost to extract it is even worth it."

"What's the big deal, Doc? If electronic equipment detects oil under the surface, what difference does the depth make? Don't they just bore down until they find it?"

"Well, as I said, Sangen, even with today's modern drills and technology, they simply cannot reach the depths of the largest known oil reserves. Plus, even though petroleum extraction has become incredibly high tech due to increased competition and the ever-escalating costs and risks involved in accessing it, these are crucial decisions that could mean the difference between being a growing profitable company or one that goes bankrupt. Did you know that depending on the depth of the oil, the average well can cost between $400,000 and $1,000,000 with absolutely no guarantee of finding any oil at all?"

"So, oleanane testing gives the exploration teams another tool to figure out the depth of the oil reserve and if it's worth the cost of going after it?"

"Right, Henry. Because flowering plants propagated and multiplied increasingly as time progressed, they naturally released more pollen and spores increasingly into the atmosphere that became part of the matrix of oil. It's then logical that the more oleanane the oil contains, the more recently the oil was formed and the closer to the earth's surface it would be found."

"So, oil from deeper depths would have much less or no oleanane at all."

"Precisely, Henry! And since the recently discovered Pennsylvania oil contains no oleanane at all, it had to have originated in a layer of the earth much deeper, before most angiosperms even existed."

"But Dr. Fred, what about the other biomarkers like vitrinite and kerogen?"

"Excellent question, Jason. Vitrinite is derived from the degradation or rotting of plants, and wood's kerogen comes from decaying marine sources like fish and plankton. Obviously, since fish and plants were around during the days of dinosaurs, both of these two compounds are commonly found in the oil, and both were present in the recent gas chromatograph testing of samples taken from the original Titusville strike back in the 1850s. However, none of these biomarkers were present in the newly discovered Titusville oil!"

"So, Dr. Fred, the basis of your hypothesis is that oil is not created by the breakdown of organic compounds at all; it's formed by the earth itself, right?"

"Yes, that's right, but remember, the abiogenic theory is not mine; I just happen to be one of many who are trying to prove it."

Dr. Fred paused just for a moment to reflect on his own arrogant naivety when he publicly refuted biogenic oil creation.

"What's up, Dr. Fred? You, OK?"

"Yes, I'm fine, Sangen. Look, I don't want to worry any of you, but I just need all of you to be aware that our work might be being monitored."

"OK, you're freaking me out, man. Monitored how? By whom and why?"

"Monitored by powerful people, Henry. Men that will use any means necessary to protect their interests. MONEY."

Imagine the impact this discovery would have on our culture, our economy, and the cost of virtually every product manufactured, not to mention how it could affect societies across the world that rely on this source of income. The net worth of billion-dollar corporations across the world could crumble. Powerful families and governments that manipulate and dictate the price of oil by controlling its production will no longer be relevant as the balance of power once maintained deep underground will shift, and the playing field will balance."

I might be a little paranoid, but I just want you all to watch your backs and not talk about our work with anyone—

not your roommates, not your friends, not your families. Actually, if any of you want to remove yourself from the group now, I would completely understand."

They paused as they processed the information, which was brief but uncomfortable. Dr. Fred was sure he would be losing one if not all of his interns after his frightening, totally unexpected warning. However, in some way, he hoped they would go voluntarily. He would rather for them all to be safe than to keep hanging around for extra credit.

After a few seconds, Sangen was the first to speak. "Uh, no way, Jose. I'm not going anywhere, Dr."

Henry was next, but he sounded far less convincing. "Uh, sure. We're here for you, doc."

Then Jason said what Fred thought Jason would say. "Yeah, dude, I'm from Brooklyn, baby! Nobody gonna mess with my homies."

"Great! Thank you so much, guys, for believing in me and what we are doing here. It means more to me than you will ever know to have this group with which I can share my crazy dream. If, I mean, WHEN we finally succeed, all of your names will be in the history books. Sorry, I mean online blogs or whatever…. But first, I will need to speak with the Board to see if we need you to sign any type of legal crap to keep our operation going."

Jason was the first to get the conversation back on track. "Cool, cool. So, doc, I know this might be way off-topic; I do have ADD, you know, but I read somewhere that during World War 2, those Nazi bastards discovered a way to manufacture petroleum in laboratories using nothing but common elements. Is that for real?"

"It's not off-topic at all, Jason. It's absolutely true, and it actually helps prove our point that oil doesn't require rotten meat or plants to be produced.

So, back during World War 2, the only fighter plane in the world with a jet engine was the Messerschmitt Bomber, and it was a crucial weapon in the Nazi's arsenal. At the height of World War 2, many raw materials like steel, rubber, and especially fuel became very scarce not just in Europe but in America as well. Just about every country involved in the war effort had enacted and enforced campaigns calling for recycling and rationing. The campaigns helped to alleviate some of the shortages and provided the factories that manufactured ammunition, weapons, planes, and vehicles, i.e., the materials they needed to continue the fight to stop Hitler. But that was helpful only up to a point."

Those Nazis you mentioned were so successful in aggressively spreading across Europe like coronavirus was largely due to their dominance in the air. The shortage of fuel threatened to ground their air force they called Luftwaffe, as well as its entire fleet of Stukas and Zeppelins. They began to utilize a process on a limited basis that could create a synthetic, high octane jet fuel. As crazy as it sounds, the synthetic fuel actually had fewer contaminants such as sulfur that are harmful to our environment. Not only that, but if synthetic fuel production was ever to ramp up again today at full-scale manufacturing, it would likely cost less per gallon than real jet fuel!

However, it wasn't the Nazis who invented the process; they just refined it. The process was first invented and patented in 1913 by another German chemist named Friedrich Bergius. Bergius discovered that by using a fine powder, adding a catalyst to it, then putting the compound under extreme heat and pressure, he could produce a stable, remarkably high-quality alternative fuel.

During WW2, the Nazi war machine relied on technology as an alternative to keep their Luftwaffe in the air and enormous Panzer tanks steamrolling across Europe. The process has been duplicated in laboratories many times since then. Actually, it has been refined even further to produce a fuel even cleaner burning and more efficient to produce than naturally occurring oil!"

"Sweet, so no dinosaurs were harmed in the making of their fuel!"

"Haha, right, Sangen. So, our job now is to find unadulterated, virgin oil before it has been contaminated by any residual organic compounds and present our finding at the next Argos Conference."

"What's the Argos Conference, doc?" asked Henry.

"The Argos Conference is an uber-exclusive, by-invitation-only group that represents the leaders of the top 100 oil producers in the world. The group meets once a month to set the real global oil forecasts, including reserve estimates and production targets. Don't ask me how I will get in, but I know what my presentation will be when I do! Well…, no pun intended; it looks like I'll be going to Pennsylvania on Monday!"

Sangen said, "But Dr. Fred, if the Argos group is all about controlling the flow of oil, why would they listen, let alone care? It seems like you might actually be putting yourself in danger just by going there."

"Good point, Sangen, and that's exactly why I warned you guys of the possibility of danger."

Over the years, I have authored books and published countless articles on this topic and have got absolutely nowhere with either the media or our own government. It's obvious that they just don't want to hear it. So, as they say, desperate times call for desperate measures. This could be a huge risk for me, but if I feel I can just get in front of the Argos group without getting myself killed before, during, or after, I will have dozens of foreign press, and government officials present that will hear my evidence and report it to the world. Taking this gamble is not only the last thing I want to do, but it's also going to be my final attempt to get the attention this matter deserves. If I can't present a credible case, or the media chooses not to run the story, I'm officially going to hang up my lab coat."

After the group had wrapped up their meeting, Fred turned the laptops off, turned off the lights, and then locked the door as he said goodbye to his interns.

A few minutes later, someone with another key to the lab returned, fired one of the laptops back up, then sent out another email from a private account.

"HE IS GOING TO TITUSVILLE, PA. WILL ARRIVE MONDAY."

Chapter 5

Driving back to campus the following day for his second day of class, Dr. Fred couldn't help feeling that the education system around the world, particularly in the United States, was a controlled, stagnant bureaucracy incapable of accepting alternative concepts—concepts that are not considered politically correct in a "clean," new world.

Before Fred, a dream team of great scientists, including Mendeleev, Berthelot, Humboldt, Smythe, and Crick, had created a Tsunami within a massive, churning cesspool. This cesspool consisted of academia, wealthy families, corporations, and governments. Each of them presented their own evidence of the abiogenic oil theory to their peers.

It didn't take long for Dr. Fred to be thrown overboard and pummeled by wave after wave of slander and humbling mockery that eventually washed over, for the most part, drowned the impressive career that took nearly 40 years for him to build. Although Ressner had been published numerous times, it was the single article he submitted to World Energy, an energy trade sector magazine, which saw his career quickly spilling away like the millions of gallons of oil that were lost at Skyview.

The powerful alignment of governments, worldwide energy-based companies, and wealthy families were all known to mercilessly attack and defend the status quo in any way necessary. These families included the Rothschilds, Burnies, and Rockefellers, along with groups including Argos, OPEC, and their well-funded subordinate activist groups like the Forest Conservation Society and the Wildlife Federation Fund.

When one of their own high-level, highly respected insiders like Dr. Fred supported alternative views by questioning the established beliefs that took generations to instill, the pushback was relentless. Utilizing media smear campaigns, litigation, and even more sinister methods were frightening enough to prevent most scientists from speaking the truth. Despite the risks, Fred chose to forge ahead.

Growing up, then returning years later to live near the beautiful, small town of Lyons, Colorado, just north of Boulder, Fred had nearly memorized every twist and turn of the narrow road just off the main highway that led to his rustic cabin. In several spots, the road was downright treacherous, especially after one of the frequent, heavy snowfalls in the mountains. Fred would often joke that he was so familiar

with these roads he could practically maneuver them blind-
folded in the dark. However, nobody ever thought it was
too funny when he pretended to do it while they were riding
along with him.

His cabin was close enough to campus but just far
enough that once he had left for the day, he wouldn't be going back. The drive gave him time to recap his day, but he
usually drifted into recalling his youth in the area where he
met his wife Kim while they were together in college. Kim,
a nature lover her entire life, became quite content with her
role and responsibilities after marriage, taking care of their
beautiful mountain home and raising their two children.

Unfortunately, after the kids had grown up and gone off
to make lives of their own, the Ressner marriage fell apart
from the unrelenting strain they endured after years of rumors and whispers that Fred was losing his mind.

Dr. Fred tried to remain as close to his two kids as possible, although they both now lived on opposite sides of the
country. But he could never quite forgive Kim for leaving
him. He felt she had abandoned him at his lowest point, for-
getting the part about "for better or worse," like so many do.
Despite her repeated efforts trying to tell him, Fred didn't realize just how bad the marriage had become until it was too
late. He had grown so distant and uncommunicative to Kim
that they had spent their last years living together, but alone.

Neither of them remarried after the divorce; the two continued to email and talk on the phone about every week, mostly about the kids and Kim's business. Ironically, they also talked about Fred's work. It was strange, but after their separation, Kim showed more interest in his research since she wasn't directly affected by it as she was during the last years of their marriage. Though Fred understood, he also inwardly resented it. But he was still eager to share the details of his work, especially with Kim.

Finally, he made it back to campus and pulled into his designated "Dr. Fred Ressner" parking space. He grabbed his laptop and backpack and began the short walk back to the auditorium for his second day of class.

"Come on, Fred, don't screw this up," he murmured to himself as he once again pulled open the double doors to the auditorium.

Chapter 6

"Good morning, everyone! How was the weekend?" said Fred, scanning the room and making a quick headcount. He was astonished to see that he wasn't missing any students, nor were there any notes that would list any kids who had dropped the class.

"Well, this is cool; everyone came back! I either have some very open-minded students, or I'm about to be canceled." Unlike his first class, today, nobody smiled, let alone bothered to muster up a smirk. Fred knew that he had to bring his A-game for today's second lecture, or there might not be the third one.

The concept of sustainable oil was not a new one, nor was it a popular one among Dr. Fred's peers. In fact, simply stating a belief in the abiogenic theory of oil creation could have meant career suicide. Yet, there he was, still trying to convert the masses like some cheap circus sideshow.

Before Fred could even begin his lecture, one of his students raised his hand as he thought to himself, *Oh crap, here we go.*

He quickly glanced at the seating chart to find the student's name and said, "Yes, sir, Mr. Riley. Riley Thompson. Do you have a question, sir?"

"Well, not so much a question but a comment. Dr. Ressner, even if oil is a naturally occurring and renewable energy resource, as you are claiming, that doesn't nullify the fact that over the last 100 years, the use of fossil fuels has caused global warming and has put the future of our planet at risk. Why would our generation or the next one ever want to use outdated technology that is destroying our climate!"

The kid didn't know it, but Fred had been playing poker with the class, and the answer to this question was his royal flush. The setup he had been waiting for even before he began teaching. Slowly, Fred nodded his head as if he agreed with the young man, then he paused, pretending to be gathering his thoughts. He then began a masterpiece lecture that was about to blow the kid's mind.

"Oh, Riley, you're referring to the Ol'anthropogenic theory, right?"

"The what?" Thompson said.

"Riley, I'm sure you would agree that if you are going to fight for a cause, you should know the real name for it, right? Anthropogenic is the name scientists have attached to global warming to make it sound more...believable. More......official. Essentially, it means manmade."

For example, the atmosphere of the Earth is made up of 78 percent nitrogen, 21 percent oxygen, .06 percent gases such as argon, and just .04 carbon dioxide. Of that .04 percent carbon dioxide, only about 1 percent is anthropogenic or manmade. So, we are told to believe by the media and government that just .0004 percent of carbon dioxide in our atmosphere is causing global warming! This is also why the United States is spending about 635 billion tax dollars a year to lower CO2, and will drastically increase spending to over 4 trillion dollars by 2035."

Follow the money, as they say, kids. This is big business; it is an entire industry designed and created to shift money and power across the globe. However, I can definitely see how all of you would think and feel the way you do. After all, you have all been spoon-fed these empty calories by your teachers, by celebrities, and from countless online sources ever since you were just little kids."

But please don't misunderstand me. I want to be perfectly clear with you. I believe in global warming. I agree it is happening. However, we can't talk about global warming without talking about global cooling, or rather the Earth continuing with what the Earth has been doing for the last hundreds of millions of years—balancing its own thermostat."

Most of us know that the Earth has had an ice age, right? But just for fun, let me ask how many of you know exactly how many ice ages the Earth has had."

The vast majority of the students said one. A few said two, and one guy in the back row said 3. Yet, it was obvious to Fred that they were all just guessing.

"We give up, Dr. How many?" Chase said.

"Well, you guys are way off except for the young man in the back. He had the closest guess of the 3. However, it's not one, two, or three. What most people don't know, because honestly, they just haven't been taught, is that the Earth has actually gone through at least five known ice age events over the past several hundred million years. Each one of these ice ages came roughly 100,000 years apart from each other. As a group, these five-ice ages are referred to as Pleistocene glaciation."

Glaciation is the period of decreasing temperatures in which ice, in some areas miles deep, slowly spreads across the planet like a ginormous icy blanket. Most people think that the glaciers that moved south toward the equator originated at the Arctic Circle. In fact, they began closer to the area around Greenland and spread south. During an ice age, the gradual but unstoppable drop in temperatures is naturally accompanied by a significant increase in ice."

Back around 1400 AD, the drastically dropping temperatures in Greenland had a profound effect on the ability of the inhabitants to grow crops and, in turn, created a food shortage. The lower temperatures led to a shortage of crops and also affected naturally growing vegetation, on which the wild animals fed. Therefore, as the natural vegetation on the island decreased, so did the wild game that the people hunted and relied on for food and clothing. The chain of events made it nearly impossible for the inhabitants there to survive, and it was one of the main reasons many of the Vikings abandoned Greenland to search for less severe climates. Many of the Vikings left the land to the more hardy Inuit, the ancestors of the Eskimo."

As temperatures continued to drop, massive ice sheets gradually spread across the region so large that they were not only capable of moving indigenous rock formations from one location to another. They were also powerful enough to form mountain ranges in some areas and flatten the Earth in others."

During every single ice age, there were also shorter periods of time of global warming called interglacial events when the massive ice sheets slowly began to melt and recede like what's happening today. The most severe ice age that we know of was the Cryogenian. It was so drastic that it virtually turned the entire Earth into a planetary snowball with glaciers so massive and powerful that over time, they continued to creep south until the ice nearly reached the equator."

Then, we have the oldest ice age that we know of, called the Huronian. This ice age was followed by the nasty Cryogenian I just spoke of. After that came the Andean-Saharan, and the Karoo. Finally, we saw the emergence of the ice age called the Quaternary, also known as the Pleistocene ice age. The Quaternary ice age period that began about 2.6 million years ago is what people, especially moviemakers in Hollywood, normally think of when they use the term Ice Age."

Riley spoke up again, "Wait, what! You are referring to the cartoon, right? Are you saying that we are still in an ice age, Dr.!"

"Yes, that's absolutely right, Riley, but I bet you've never heard the local weather people talk about it, huh? You've got to ask yourself why that is. As a matter of fact, there is a lot of information they don't tell you."

"Like what, Dr. Fred?"

"Well, how about this. Did any of you know that the ozone layer over the Antarctic is nearly closed today despite the inconvenient truth that China is now using more chlorofluorocarbons than ever? When the Montreal Protocol was enacted in the 1970s, it significantly reduced the amount of the so-called ozone-depleting chemicals. These chemicals were once widely used across the world as refrigerants, cleaners, and aerosol propellants. These materials did indeed appear to have an effect as the hole slowly began closing. Today, however, not only is the hole nearly completely closed, the use of CFS has been gradually increasing for decades now."

Anyway, let's get back to the ice age. Between 10,000 and 25,000 years ago, the planet began warming, and we have been slowly phasing into a warmer period of interglaciation within the current ice age. Around 50 million years ago, when we were smack dab in the middle of our current ice age, the sea level was around 400 feet lower than it is today. This was mainly because the ice was drawn from the oceans and seas and deposited over vast areas of land."

Then, during another interglacial period that began around 125,000 years ago, the sea level went from minus 400 feet to about 18 feet above our current levels. Think about that. Today every major city near an ocean or sea would be under water! Today, scientists are pouring gas on fire but guess what? There were no factories or automobiles churning out CO2 to make the Earth warmer during a single interglacial period of ANY recorded ice age event. Make no mistake. We are, in fact, living in the Quaternary ice age."

On a side note, don't worry. This won't be on your tests. I recall spending time with some cousins in Southern Indiana near a little town called Madison one summer when I was a kid. Since we didn't have video games and only three television channels back then, we had to find other ways to entertain ourselves."

"Oh, brutal man. What did you do for fun?"

"Well, we spent most days playing outside, riding bikes, hiking, exploring. Since it was Indiana, we played a lot of basketball.

Anyway, one day while out exploring with my cousins, we decided to hike down an old, abandoned railroad line that had been literally blasted and carved out of a hillside creating a long, steep incline that led a couple of miles down to the Ohio River. Barges would bring goods into the port of Madison. From there, the trains would transport those goods from the river, up the rails, cut into the hillside, and then onto who knows where."

During our hikes down that railroad cut, we found dozens, maybe hundreds of fossilized ocean creatures like the Goniasma, the Orthopnea, and the Pseudo Melania. I was just a kid, maybe 12 or 13 years old. Yet still, I always wondered just how in the hell these tiny sea creatures got all the way to Indiana, died, and were buried under tons of clay, rocks, and dirt, ultimately becoming fossilized."

Years later, when I was in my 20s and earned a degree in geology, I learned that at the end of an ice age around 3 million years ago, the sea level was a whopping 150 to 175 feet higher than it is today. Again, imagine for a moment Indiana and the entire American Midwest were completely under seawater! I also learned that the temperature of our planet has been a fluid, moving target since the beginning of time.

Today, scientists continue to tell us the sky is falling even though it is an event that is completely out of our hands. We can ban all the chemicals and fossil fuels in the world right now. At the end of the day, our planet is not only enormous but also self-healing, and it will continue to do exactly what it has been doing for hundreds of millions of years. Regulate itself.

In fact, when you do an online search on climate change, you will notice there are dozens of websites that will tell you that estimated sea level increases could be anywhere between 2 inches and 20 feet over the next 100 years. Seriously! 2 INCHES to 20 FEET? Kids, these brilliant, well-funded scientists really have no clue.

Geesh, I'm sorry, I got off track. As I was saying, we know that periods of global warming come intermittingly during the ice ages. They always come at the end of them. However, the warming period we are experiencing now is nowhere close to what we will see when our current ice age finally does come to an end. We can only pray that it will pale in comparison to the drastic warming event that occurred at the end of the Andean-Saharan ice age. This warming makes today's period of warming seem like a cool day at the beach.

In fact, in 2021, this very university published an article in Science Daily stating that during the previous interglacial period, around 125,000 years ago, the temperature had increased so much that the area within the Arctic Circle was green and lush with hundreds of varieties of shrubs, flowering plants, and even dwarf Aspen trees. The researchers discovered that the temperature in the Arctic was somewhere around nine degrees warmer than today. This weather pattern remained until the Earth eventually began to cool again.

Between the last two ice age events, dinosaurs, along with countless other plant and animal species, thrived in areas well above the Arctic Circle. This was proven by the discovery of fossils in the region. They believe that at one time, some areas of the Arctic Circle were actually densely forested with abundant amounts of diverse plants and animal life."

A hand quickly went up, this time to ask a question.

"So, Dr. Ressner, I think you know that most of us in your class are opposed to the use of fossil fuels. But if man and fossil fuels weren't responsible for the warming periods hundreds of thousands, if not millions of years ago, then what was the cause?"

"Thank you for asking! I can say that I'm 100% positive that it was not due to cars, factories, airplanes, or dinosaur farts. The combination of events that must occur to move our planet out of an ice age event and toward a period of interglaciation is still in play today. They are all woven together by a single common thread that begins with a very slight variation in the tilt and orbit of the Earth around the sun. This affects how much sunlight hits the Northern Hemisphere during the summer months. We know this because every documented ice age event has begun in the Northern Hemisphere. In reality, the Southern Hemisphere and Antarctica have remained relatively unaffected by warming."

For whatever reason, the media and government don't want you to know this. Were any of you aware that since the 1970s, the ice caps in the South Pole have increased in size? Even more importantly, the average annual temperature at the South Pole has actually decreased during this same period of time. This is only a hypothesis, but to me, this indicates we are now on the threshold of a major period of interglaciation warming that could last for thousands of years and be absolutely devastating to the world as we now know it.

In other words, class, it will be getting much warmer. Despite what you are hearing, reading, and being fed on a daily basis, there is absolutely nothing man can do about it. Even if every fossil-fuel-burning engine and power plant in the world ceased to exist tomorrow, the temperature would continue to rise unless there is another change in the tilt of the Earth. When it eventually happens, this tilt will then send us in the opposite direction once again."

At this point, most of the class had that deer in the headlight look as if they were either scared or just couldn't process the information.

"As I was saying, the variations in the Earth's tilt and orbit create a devastating chain reaction. First, the reflective ice, which typically sends the sun's radiative heat back up, is reduced. This allows even more heat to be absorbed by the Earth. This is known as the albedo effect, and yes, that WILL be on your test.

Next, as the warming of the earth increases, water from our seas and oceans will begin to evaporate faster, causing more water vapors, another type of greenhouse gas. Then, as the temperature continues to rise, the permafrost begins to thaw and allows ground cover such as peat, moss, and grass to decompose, releasing even more methane into the atmosphere."

In case you didn't know this fact, methane is naturally released by decaying vegetation and has a warming effect that is 80 times greater than the CO_2 released from your car's engine!

Finally, as ocean temperatures continue to rise, the cycle of higher biological growth and death occurs in not only fish and mammals but also plankton, seaweed, and algae. The propagation of all of these species and organisms followed by their decomposition causes an even greater amount of methane to be released into the atmosphere."

"Dr. I read that some scientists had proposed making cattle ranchers place some kind of devices on their cows' butts to capture their farts. No pun intended, but even I think that's bullshit!"

For the first time that he could ever remember, Fred let out a belly laugh so hard that his students couldn't help but laugh right along with him.

"Well, I call that bovine scatology. BS! For short," Dr. Fred joked.

"Actually, guys, all joking aside, let me state the facts. Since our planet is composed of about 70% water and only around 30% land, more methane gas is produced and released into the atmosphere from the seas and oceans than from every single living thing on land combined!"

Scientists across the world go on to ignore these facts while they continue to publish reports of doom and gloom and our impending fate. All the while, they reap billions of dollars in funding condemning man's use of fossil fuels. Not to mention the old saying in the news business that bad news sells more newspapers than good news."

"Oh, yeah, I've heard of newspapers."

"Haha, very funny. Come on now. I'm not THAT old! Class, all I ask is that you think for yourselves and form your own decisions. Believe me, I understand peer pressure at your age and the worldwide cancel culture environment we are living in. But try to look through the constant bombardment of propaganda to form your own opinions and be leaders, not followers."

Not long ago, an online petition was drawn up that urged the United States to reject manmade global warming and the Kyoto protocol. The petition went viral as over 31,000 scientists from around the world signed it, including Piers Corbyn, one of the leading physicists in the world. Dr. Corbyn began recording weather patterns in the early 1950s when he was just five years old."

"Geesh, Dr. Fred, and I thought you had a boring childhood."

"Hahaha, good one. Mr. Corbyn was a child prodigy and had published a significant amount of evidence agreeing with John Coleman, the late great founder of the Weather Chanel. He agreed that manmade global warming is a false theory. The man is brilliant, yet, when you look at his profile on Wikipedia, he is described as a conspiracy theorist. This is a blatant attempt to discredit him in order to make his life's work seem irrelevant."

Another example of a campaign of smear and cancel tactics has been directed at one of the most influential think tanks in the world. I'm sure all of you know what think tanks are, right? These are groups of incredibly intelligent scientists dedicated to the truth who work together to solve some of our world's most challenging problems. There is one such think tank called the CATO Institute, whose scientists wrote to then-President Obama. They wrote that his view on manmade climate change was critically flawed and drastically overstated. However, of course, the media went straight to work, and the CATO report was swiftly labeled as a fringe right-wing conspiracy group."

The thought that crude oil is a naturally occurring by-product of the Earth and is as abundant as the water is just too far from common beliefs. Or, more accurately, too far from their funding for western academic elitists to even consider. The common, more popular theory of the past 60 years has been the biogenic formation of oil."

Biogenic simply means that petroleum was created from biological matter such as rotting plants and animals, an idea that was first proposed by Georg Agricola over 400 years ago. Since the 1960s, every kid who went through high school was taught this theory. At the same time, the idea somehow gained backing from governments and universities across the world. They continue to hold onto the ancient theory like an old wives' tale. Even though, to date, there have been well over 4,000 published documents and manuscripts submitted from around the world, offering scientific proof and refuting the biogenic theory of oil creation."

Advances in modern testing equipment and methods have provided more than enough evidence showing that oil is not made from rotting organic matter at all. Rather it is produced many miles underground, likely somewhere between the core and mantle at incredibly high temperatures and pressures. Similar to the conditions required to turn a lump of dirty black carbon into a beautiful diamond, the same process can also create oil."

Being a geologist for nearly my entire life, I know that even with all the high-tech equipment available to us today, we still don't know what the exact composition of the mantle of the planet really is. We have theorized what we think might be down there based on the analysis of the data of shock waves that occur after earthquakes. We also have precious and rare earth minerals that are spewed from active volcanoes. However, we have no other real proof. There could be Fruity Pebbles down there for all we know."

In March 2020, an article was published by Live Science. The article stated that two large blobs were discovered lurking within the mantle of the Earth. Most scientists will admit they have no idea what these massive blobs are, but I have a fairly good idea they are seeing the birth of oil!"

For over a hundred years, scientists from around the world who have disputed the theory of biogenic oil formation have become victims of cancel culture. Even earlier than that, around the year 1800, a geologist from Germany named Alexander Von Humboldt was one of the first contrarians. He was the inventor of a method of measuring barometric pressure that is still used today in weather forecasting. He was one of the most famous men in Europe at that time."

Later, there was Pierre Berthelot of France. He was one of the most respected chemists of the late 1800s and the inventor of the first synthetic oil created without any organic compounds. He used a simple combination of common elements."

In addition to these two men, probably the most accomplished of them all was Mendeleev of Russia. Mendeleev was seen by many as the Russian prototype of a young, upcoming Einstein in America. He was a supremely respected scientist with a cult-like following. He had near-celebrity status and was also the creator of the periodic table of elements."

Most recently, a couple of old, close friends of mine, Dr. Thomas Smythe of England, along with his colleague Dr. Francis Crick, have continued to carry the abiogenic torch. It is their relentlessly brave efforts to re-educate the world about the true theory of oil creation."

Make no mistake, finding pure, untainted oil in its natural state without any trace of biological compounds is not an easy task. However, it has been done before, actually several times."

In 1997, NASA launched the space probe Cassini. After traveling for seven years and nearly 100 million miles through the cold, silent vacuum of deep space, it eventually began transmitting bizarre data back to Earth that it had gathered from Titan, one of the 82 moons of Saturn. It turned out the Cassini probe had discovered that Titan contained liquid hydrocarbons. Oil on its surface! Not just a little oil, but over 100 times the total amount of all known reserves on Earth combined."

Although not a single living plant or animal has ever been known to have existed on the moon Titan, it is virtually saturated with the oil!"

That's not the first report of extra-terrestrial hydrocarbons that have been found. When a meteorite called ALH 84001 originating from Mars was found back in the same year, scientists discovered that it also had organic-free polycyclic aromatic hydrocarbons, Oil!"

We can even traverse closer in time, like Michael J Fox in his DeLorean, to the 1940s. In the distant past, we find Nobel Prize-winning chemist and head of England's Royal Society Sir Robert Robinson stating that 'Oil appears to be nothing more than a primordial substance in which biological byproducts have been added.'"

In other words, oil is created deep within the Earth, and then it carries these organic biomarkers with it as it migrates up through the cracks in the Earth's crust."

I'm going to stray off-topic for a minute or two by sharing with you the story of Samuel Keir. I told my interns earlier today. Since many of you have a passion for saving the planet as you should, what would you say if I told you that oil also probably saved the sperm whale from certain extinction?"

Electric lighting, which we take for granted today, didn't exist until Swan and Edison made their breakthrough discovery in 1880. Before then, up to the mid-1800, whale blubber was widely used as a cheap source of fuel to light lanterns at the time. After years of over-harvesting the whales for their blubber, they were on the verge of extinction. Then, in 1848, a man named Samuel Kier came up with an idea. Kier, who owned a salt mining company in Pennsylvania, began distilling the sticky tar into kerosene."

It was a nice little side hustle business. Plus, it helped him reduce the amount of sticky tar that was threatening his salt mining company. Knowing the tar could burn, Kier began to market the product as a cheap replacement for whale blubber."

With help from Edwin Drake of Titusville, Pennsylvania, the first man to drill for oil in America, the two-man team was able to significantly increase production. Eventually, Kier constructed the first oil refinery in the country in Pittsburg. Kier successfully saved his salt mine and went on to make a fortune distilling oil. Neither man was ever given the credit they deserved for saving the sperm whale."

But I digress. Around 70 years later and a few thousand miles across the country, the first major oil strike in the state of California, and still one of the largest finds in our country's history, was discovered by a man nicknamed Dry Hole Pete at the Skyview well."

"Oh, now I get it, professor, your last lecture on Dry Hole Pete has something to do with oil as a renewable energy source because it's actually made by the Earth!"

"Yes! You got it! Today's sophisticated testing methods weren't available at the time. However, samples were taken of that original oil from Skyview, and they still exist today. When the old samples were eventually tested, all of the biomarkers vitrinite, kerogen, and oleanane were found in them. Eventually, when just a single giant derrick running 24 hours a day finally pumped out the last barrel of oil, the Skyview well was capped and left dry."

Recently, the dry field of Skyview has now somehow become replenished with oil. This is only possible when oil migrates either from another horizontal field, which in this case, there are none. Or, from miles below the surface of the Earth, up through cracks and fissures, until it finally finds its way to massive underground reservoirs where it is held. Then, it remains in storage until it is eventually discovered. Incredibly, the new oil now being pumped from the ground at Skyview contains none of the biomarkers the original oil had. It doesn't contain vitrinite, it doesn't contain kerogen, and it doesn't contain oleanane."

"Dr. Fred, the basis of your lecture and this class is that oil is not created by the breakdown of organic compounds at all, but it is formed by the Earth itself, right?"

"Yes, that's correct."

"Well, isn't this enough data to prove that biogenic oil formation is a false theory?"

"One would think so. As I mentioned, when oil migrates through the Earth's crust, it usually finds its way into enormous underground reservoirs. During its time in storage, it naturally picks up many organic, non-petroleum-based substances. When scientists analyze the oil and find these substances called biomarkers, they mistakenly theorized that since the oil has them, they must have also been the source of its creation."

A young lady in Fred's class said, "That's like saying that since seawater holds salt, then salt must have created the seawater!"

"Bravo, young lady! There you have it, ladies and gentlemen. After just two classes, you are now thinking more logically than about 99% of the scientists claiming that we are going to run out of oil. Also, those scientists who are under the fallacy that by using fossil fuels, we are causing global warming."

Since the new oil at Skyview was under such tremendous pressure, it had rushed up through the Earth from the core/mantle interface and up through its crust. It went so quickly that there wasn't time for it to dwell in the reservoirs and become contaminated. Plus, the reservoirs were likely washed of all of the original organic biomarkers after it was first pumped dry by Dry Hole Pete."

Riley Thompson spoke up for the last time, "I must say, Dr. Fred, I'm kind of blown away right now. I was totally about to drop this crazy class, but now I kind of want to see where it goes."

"That's great, Riley, but like last week I've gone way over my time again. I'll see you guys again on Wednesday."

Madison, Indiana railroad cuts

Chapter 7

From the late 1800s to the early 1900s, many brilliant German chemists and engineers have been recognized for their incredible scientific contributions. Their work was so advanced that they are still widely used today. Rudolph Diesel created his namesake diesel engine in 1896.

Felix Hoffmann, while working for the Bayer company, invented aspirin in 1897. Benz and Daimler invented the automobile in 1886. Gummy bears, adhesive tape, and even the helicopter all originated during this time in Germany. Even Albert Einstein, who most Americans unknowingly identify as one of their own, also migrated from Germany. Einstein brought with him the equation and theory of $E=MC^2$. Without this equation, the ability to create and control manmade nuclear fusion might still not exist today.

Also, among the illustrious German immigrants to America is a former SS member of the Nazi party, Wernher Von Braun. He is often mistakenly considered by some to be the father of NASA. It is argued that Von Braun had actually used mathematical equations from American physicist Robert Goddard, the inventor of the first liquid-fueled rocket.

After working for Hitler and the SS division of the Nazis, Von Braun fled Germany during World War 2 and made his way to the United States. He spent several years proving his allegiance to his new home country, not to mention being watched very closely by the United States government. Von Braun was eventually named director of NASA's Marshall Space flight program.

Following the fall of the Nazi Empire, the next wave of great scientists was ready to step up and fill the void. In Europe in the 1950s and the post-World War 2 era, two young Englishmen were about to emerge as dominant forces in multiple fields of science. Both would have significant careers lasting for decades to come. Dr. Francis Crick and his colleague, Dr. Thomas Smythe, were both well-known as brilliant mathematicians. However, it was their belief in abiogenic oil formation that had made them both equally notorious.

Spending countless hours in laboratories, Crick is credited with identifying the structure of DNA. To this day, DNA is still referenced as the building block of all discoveries in genetics. He had achieved near rockstar status, almost unheard of in the world of science, with a few exceptions such as Einstein, Dr. Nye the Science Guy, and Neil deGrasse Tyson. However, unlike those men, Crick had also been labeled as somewhat of a playboy. A reputation he wasn't delighted with but grudgingly accepted as part of his persona.

A steadfast bachelor, Dr. Crick took great satisfaction in intentionally annoying his fellow colleagues. He did this by hosting countless extravagant parties that were often attended by high-profile guests, including athletes and high-ranking politicians. Even some lesser-known musicians and B-list entertainers could be seen at his parties. However, his competitors never made the invitation lists.

It was as if he was the prototype for the fictional movie hero James Bond. Ian Fleming, coincidentally also an Englishman, would create this iconic character at around the same time Crick was in his prime. However, Crick was more than just a social butterfly. He was a sophisticated party animal, holding as many events at his sprawling estate just outside of London as time would allow. The definition of an extrovert, he found tremendous satisfaction in showing off his stunning mansion and mingling with his guests.

It was common seeing Crick at one of his lavish parties with a martini in one hand and a trophy girl in the other. He was often surrounded by a group of much younger women. However, his friends Smythe and Ressner could never figure out how.

Crick wasn't tall or athletic and had thinning salt and pepper hair. He gave Ressner and Smythe hope as women would gravitate and hang onto his every word with anticipation. They carefully listened to his elaborate yet mostly embellished stories of travels around the world. They would, at times, appear to be hypnotized as they would listen to the incredible adventures he had encountered on his journeys. He often sounded more like Indiana Jones than James Bond.

However, Crick was much less humble. His in-your-face style and overly confident personality certainly seemed to irritate a lot of starched collars that were already buttoned up much too tightly. His behavior also contributed to his more groundbreaking discoveries being always challenged, if not outright rejected, by his colleagues. That is at least up until the point he was proven right.

Alternately, referring to them as either jealous nerds or scurvy ravens, he loved watching them competing for second place. He was amused as they would jockey for recognition and compete with one another for attention and tenure by stealing each other's theories only to present them as their own.

Sometimes he would stoop to the level of the spiteful little man that resorted to openly mocking others. Crick could be rather harsh as he belittled his peers in public after a few vodka martinis. He would quote, somewhat loosely, his favorite speech from Theodore Roosevelt.

"It is not the critic who counts. No, not the man too afraid to throw his hat into the ring to compete but would rather sit on the sidelines in comfort only to point out the flaws and weaknesses of the fighter. But without the fighter who sacrificed and risked everything for a greater prize, there would be nothing left for the fearful critic to complain about."

Of course, this further agitated his second-rate colleagues. In reality, boldly flexing his confidence served a slightly higher purpose of impressing his younger female companions.

Despite his brash, almost combative behavior, his friends Dr. Smythe and the much younger Dr. Ressner both admired their gifted friend. Once Crick's performance to the small group was over, his friends came forward.

"Bravo, sir!" Smythe said to Crick as he gave his long-time friend a bear hug.

"Good evening Dr., the house looks absolutely magnificent. I see you not only possess a keen wit but by the look
of the guests surrounding you also still have a very impressive little black book as well."

Crick laughed at Smythe's little black book reference,
"Sir, please. I have not had a black book since 1999. I now
have Facebook and Instagram! But I'm glad you like the
remodel, Thomas. Next week, I have the entire kitchen gut-
ted. You know you just can't entertain in style without a real
chef's kitchen. It's going to be spectacular! It should. It's
costing me a small fortune!"

Then, abruptly and in the same breath, Crick became
uncharacteristically restrained. His face was nearly frozen,
and his voice became nearly inaudible as he stared directly
into his friends' eyes.

"Thomas, do you recognize that man standing near the
back door? Is he one of our colleagues that I have forgotten
over the years? A member of the press, perhaps?"

Smythe first thought that his friend was playing a joke
on him. However, after noticing the expression on Crick's
face, Smythe decided to play along and casually turned to
glance in the direction of the man.

"No, Francis, I don't think I have ever seen him before. Maybe he's just a party crasher trying to snatch up some of your leftovers."

"Yes, I suppose so."

Smythe and Ressner couldn't understand why Crick had suddenly become so visibly shaken, and his usual light-hearted demeanor had immediately become much more intense. It was concerning them both. It was pretty clear that the fear in his shaky voice and the worry on his face were not going anywhere. Both men tried to reassure Crick that everything was OK.

"Francis, I'm sure he's harmless. Would you like Fred and me to go over and speak with him? Maybe rough him up a bit?"

Smythe laughed and said, smiling, "No, no. I'm sure your right, Tom. It's just...I swear I have seen him around several times the last week or so, and now he's in my home. I'm sure your right, though, Thomas. He doesn't appear to be too sinister. I suppose it's just my imagination playing tricks on me. Just make sure he doesn't drink all the bloody vodka. Let's just forget about him and have a good night, shall we? Now, gentlemen, I'm late for my checkup with Dr. Ink. Who else needs a fresh martini?"

Being a mathematician and spending most of his time in laboratories, Thomas Smythe was usually a very analytical man. He was analytical to a fault, as he seemed to be distant and uninterested in the problems or feelings of other people. However, as he continued to dwell on the worried demeanor of his good friend, he became more uncomfortable himself and acted completely out of character. He grabbed Dr. Fred by the arm and said, "Come with me, Fred; let's go say hello to our little friend."

Fred knew Smythe was looking out for his friend. And at that moment, he smiled as he remembered what Jason had said to him in the lab.

"Nobody messes with my homies."

At first glance, the man didn't appear to Smythe or Ressner to be out of place. Standing about 6 ft 3 inches tall and with an obvious muscular build, the man wore a fitted black suit with a black vest and a slim black tie. He looked pretty much just like all the other well-dressed guests. However, there was one exception. The gun holster hidden under his jacket could be seen when he moved at a certain angle.

Smythe and Ressner began making their way down the winding staircase, leaning on an intricate hand-carved mahogany banister that led them to the vast, imported Italian marble floor.

Gently nudging their way through the maze of bodies, they were only about 10 feet away from the uninvited stranger when he casually opened the back door and slithered outside. Just a split second before he made it out the door, Ressner caught a brief glimpse of the gun and what appeared to be the top of an oddly designed tattoo on the top left side of the man's neck.

Out of place for this crowd, Ressner thought to himself.

When the two had finally made it to the back door, they quickly pulled it open and prepared to confront the man outside on the expansive back patio hand paved in beautiful imported Spanish slate. Yet, there was nobody there. He had seemingly vanished into the misty, frigid night air.

"Fred, whoever that guy was, he was obviously in a hurry to leave. Maybe Francis was right."

"Yeah, Thomas. That wasn't normal whatsoever."

As the two men composed themselves to come back inside and rejoin the party, they were both now genuinely concerned though they were trying to hide it from their friend. Crick was still perched on the balcony and noticed what his friends had done. From the balcony and across the crowded room, he made eye contact with them both. Then, he threw both his hands up and mouthed, "WTF!"

Crick was now even more convinced that he was being stalked. Having a stalker was frightening, but not knowing why or by who scared the hell out of him even more.

Chapter 8

Thomas Smythe was a highly regarded and prestigious astrophysicist who arguably had a career even more impressive than his friends Dr. Crick and Ressner—a career so broad that it seemed to make most scientists, including his friends, look like underachievers.

Knowing each other for so many years and sharing many common beliefs and personality traits allowed them to go months without talking and then strike up a meaningful conversation without missing a beat. With no jealousy, competition, or envy between the three, they had all remained close friends for decades. Although Smythe wasn't the partying type, he rarely missed one of his friends' events just for the sheer entertainment value. He would usually just find an empty spot in a corner and enjoy Crick's uncanny ability as he would hold the attention of anyone that would listen or to anyone who couldn't find a polite way to walk away. His exhausting gift of gab could go for hours on end.

Smythe had worked in the highest reaches of science and had even been promoted to the position of overseeing the design, construction, and operation of the world's largest radio telescope, the National Astronomy and Ionosphere center located in Arecibo, Puerto Rico.

Commissioned by the United States Department of Defense as part of an early missile warning system, the telescope's other initially undisclosed and mysterious purpose was also to detect any faint radio signals originating from deep space, hoping to intercept some type of alien communication signal at first contact. The 1000-foot diameter dish was placed partially submerged in a massive sinkhole located in the northwest region of Puerto Rico. It was the largest radioscope of its kind in the world until 2020 when two of its main support cables snapped. Eventually, more cables would break, causing the massive dish to collapse into the sinkhole below. In addition to its intended purposes, the site was also so visually impressive that during its time in operation, it was often used in filming several major motion pictures, including GoldenEye, Species, and Contact.

When it came to personal conflicts, unlike his friend Crick who seemed to enjoy them, Smythe chose not to engage in petty tit-for-tat arguments with his critics. He felt it much easier on his irritable bowel and high blood pressure to simply ignore them with profound indifference. In 1969, when a reporter asked a young Dr. Smythe about the upcoming mission to the moon, he was incorrectly quoted as saying that the first astronauts might sink into a bottomless pit of moon dust. Fake news that he could have allowed festering inside him for years like a pesky parasite, but it seemingly had no adverse effect whatsoever on his prolific career successes to come.

Though, like Crick, Smythe was also considered a maverick, a rebel in his field. He was well known not only for fully supporting the abiogenic formation of oil but for many years, he was also one of the most internationally acclaimed and outspoken proponents of the theory. Smythe found a sadistic pleasure in giving smart-ass answers to the irritatingly mundane, scripted questions of newspaper, magazine, and television reporters. He also got his kicks by finding ways of shifting the conversation to his narrative of abiogenic oil at any opportunity he could. Over the years, he had grown to be even more enthusiastic and outspoken about this subject than just about any of his previous works. In light of his belief that the entire world had been intentionally lied to for decades, Smythe had made it a personal crusade to get the word out as wherever, whenever, and however he could.

Dr. Ressner had an extensive knowledge of geology and chemistry that led to his support of abiogenic oil. The foundation of Smythe's belief was based primarily on his extensive awareness of astrophysics and the incredible discoveries of petroleum on several other planets and moons within our own solar system, including on Mars, Jupiter, and the moon Titan. Planets that were believed to be nothing more than lifeless rocks yet held vast reserves of hydrocarbons.

Smythe was once quoted, accurately this time, saying, "The human race has endured many self-inflicted wounds over the millennia, but the perpetuation of the global conspiracy to literally enslave the entire world population by controlling the world's energy may be one of its greatest travesties." His radical statement was intentionally designed to draw more attention to the matter than anything else.

When several of his more outspoken rivals finally challenged Smythe to put his money where his mouth was and prove the theory, Smythe came through with a daring gamble that, if it backfired, would have destroyed him.

After presenting a compelling case on abiogenic oil creation to the Swedish government, even Smythe was astonished when he successfully persuaded the Swedes to set up an operation that would have a team drill over 6 kilometers into a solid granite vein, hoping to strike oil. Since granite begins as a molten semi-liquid similar to lava and formed at extreme temperatures, any organic substances would have been vaporized without a trace. Smythe theorized that the micro-fissures that ran vertically up through the granite would prevent any horizontal or ground-level compounds from contaminating it. This meant that the only oil they would find could only have come from more than six miles deep. Much deeper than oil has ever been recovered from and much deeper than any land-based oil rig has ever drilled.

When Ressner heard of Smythe's plan, he called Thomas before he left for Sweden and said, "This will be the final nail in the biogenic coffin Thomas. I wish you the best of luck, my friend."

With backing from a small group of private equity investors who believed in him and, more importantly, were hoping to profit, Smythe and the Swedish team successfully extracted six barrels of pure, unadulterated crude oil out of the solid granite. Fortunately, for Dr. Smythe, once the extracted oil was analyzed by the Swedish government, it was found to contain no trace of organic compounds typically found in the oil, proving that it had to be created by the Earth itself.

The lack of horizontal fractures and crevices in the granite had allowed the oil to migrate from deep within the Earth's mantle near its core and then up closer to its crust.

After the results of the test came in, Smythe could finally and proudly proclaim to the group of Swedish scientists, "Gentlemen, I give you the blood of the earth!"

Once news of Smythe's astounding experiments had spread, the Soviet government almost immediately duplicated his tests and confirmed his finding by drilling over 300 holes into the Swedish granite.

Smythe had another notch on his calculator that he hoped would further piss off his critics, but he was feeling old. He had been chasing prestigious projects around the world for decades, and it had taken a toll. Smythe was running on fumes and adrenaline but also feeling like he was on top of the world when he boarded the helicopter that took him from the drill site back to his hotel in Stockholm.

Unfortunately, the feeling of euphoria didn't last long. While in midflight, a journalist from the BBC in England called asking him for a statement regarding the mysteriously gruesome murder of his friend Francis Crick. The news shocked Smythe, and he felt as if the granite he had just drilled into had fallen on top of him.

He struggled to find the words, but they just wouldn't come out. As the reporter continued, he could only hear Smythe gasping for air, stuttering, and making unintelligible sounds on the other end of the phone.

"Sir, are you OK? Doctor Smythe, is this the first you've heard this news? Hello?" Smythe was simply unable to speak. He turned his phone off, dropped it onto the floor of the helicopter, and slowly lowered his head and cried until the helicopter landed near his hotel.

Learning of a close friend's murder was the kind of news that nobody could ever be prepared for or immediately respond to. It affected Smythe to the point of making him physically ill. He at once lost any feeling of happiness and desire to celebrate his discovery.

Arriving back at his hotel, the physically and emotionally exhausted man collapsed on the bed in his room before forcing himself up to soak in a hot bath with Epsom salts.

Trying to take his mind off Crick, he self-medicated with a couple of shots of Kentucky bourbon and a Xanax, then watched some mind-numbing television. The kind where you didn't even have to think because the laugh tracks told you it was supposed to be funny.

None of this was working, though, as his mind continued to race, thinking to himself, *Who the hell would want to kill Francis? And why?* He then remembered the man at Crick's party that he and Ressner tried to chase down.

Eventually, overwhelming thoughts of one scenario or another began swirling and circling around his mind like his bathwater going down the drain. The horrible thoughts were soon replaced by exhaustion and the pain in his aching body.

He had nearly drifted asleep when his phone rang again, this time startling Smythe, causing him to spill his drink. "For God's sake, what now! If this is another damn reporter, I'm going to lose my shit!"

When he picked the phone up from the side table next to the bed, the caller ID showed the call was coming from Cambridge, Massachusetts, just across the Charles River from Boston.

Smythe knew exactly what and who was in Cambridge, and he fought the urge to ignore the call. He reluctantly answered, "Hello, Smythe here."

On the other end of the call was the newly appointed Dean of the school of business at one of the most prestigious Ivy League schools in America. The type of academic institution he, Crick, and Ressner all detested but found themselves somewhat held hostage by the necessary evil as they frequently funded their adventures when private investors wouldn't.

In a thick, English accent, the caller spoke, "Good evening Dr. Smythe. This is Andrew Horine; how the hell are you, sir?"

"Horine? I thought you were still over at Oxford. What the bloody hell are you doing in Boston!"

"Please, don't hold it against me, Thomas, but you know how it goes when they pull up with a dump truck full of money and park it at your feet. It's hard to say no!"

"Yeah, I'm sure it is. What can I do for you, Andrew?" Before Horine could even speak, Smythe had already decided to pass on whatever it was Horine was selling.

They had known each other since their prep school days, and Smythe remembered Horine as a scrawny, unpopular kid who always thought he was the smartest guy in the room. A yes man and expert ass kisser who would throw his momma from a train if it meant getting himself a step ahead. He never considered them to be friends and was surprised when he called, but Horine proceeded to lay out the reason for his call that night.

"Thomas, we are hosting an important event to raise money."

"Of course, you are Horine. It seems it doesn't matter how much money there is. It's just never enough for you people, is it?"

Horine could hear the detest and resentment in Smythe's voice, but what he didn't know was that Smythe was not only physically exhausted from his trip, but he was emotionally wiped out after hearing the news of his friend's death.

"Thomas, please hear me out. I truly apologize for any past differences we've had, mate, but this isn't about the university or me. This is one of the biggest fundraisers of the year for us. 100% of the donations we collect during this event will go directly to inner-city and rural school programs in the United States. Our goal is to fund 100 schools for an entire year with free breakfast for those in need, free laptops, and after-school care for kids whose mums and dads must work late.

"Tom, it's a massively ambitious project. What do you say, mate? Would you please consider it? We have many prominent donors who have requested your presence. You may not know this, Thomas, but in our circles, it seems your reputation as a maverick innovator is quite appealing to wealthy American entrepreneurs. What say, you sir? Will you join us?"

Wanting to pass on the invitation simply because of who had offered it, Smythe hesitated before considering the cause. After a brief pause to think, he took another big gulp of Kentucky bourbon. He had hoped that the burning sensation in his throat would make the phone call more palatable.

Smythe then said, "Well, Andrew, perhaps after I bury my best friend who was murdered yesterday, I suppose I can find the time to help you."

"Oh Christ, Thomas, I had no idea. Why didn't you tell me?"

"Because you didn't ask me, you selfish wanker!"

Horine tried to feel bad for Thomas, but it just wasn't in his nature. "Thomas, I am terribly sorry. If you can't make it next week, I completely understand."

Smythe paused for a moment, realizing that Horine didn't even ask who it was that was killed. Then, he eventually agreed to accept the invitation mainly because he believed that the purpose was larger than his own depression, ego, or his dislike for Horine.

"Fantastic, Thomas! I will email the committee and inform them to prepare your itinerary. This will only be a press-the-flesh cocktail party. You will not be required to speak, only to come and be your charming self."

"Goodnight, Horine."

As Smythe swiped the END button on his cell phone as hard and fast as he could to hang up on Horine, he wished that he still had an old-fashioned landline phone. The kind that you could slam down so hard the caller could hear just how angry you were and not just whimper away by sliding the END CALL button.

Chapter 9

The first-class flight that began his all-expenses-paid trip to Boston arrived at Logan International mid-afternoon on a Friday. Spotting the name SMYTHE on a large poster near the luggage claim area, the limo chauffeured him to the uber-luxurious Beacon hotel that oozed in a style that Dr. Smythe wasn't accustomed to. He couldn't help but think of the absurd irony of the unbelievable expense he had been provided compared to the stark contrast of the kids he was there to help.

"Why can't these bloody American bastards just get out their checkbooks rather than demanding on a show before they are willing to help anyone?"

Still fatigued from his trip to Sweden, Smythe knew he needed to change his attitude and fast. Once he was checked in, a bellhop carried his luggage for him, and they made their way up to his penthouse suite.

After generously tipping the young man, he tried settling down for a quick nap before the main event but couldn't seem to switch off his swirling mind. He once again began thinking about the loss of his old friend. For a moment, he considered easing the depression he was feeling by calling Fred, but he shrugged it off. Thinking that talking more about it might make him even more miserable than he already was.

He then decided to focus his thoughts on what would become his next obsession. Another radical theory he had been working on for several years.

Smythe was convinced that all life existing at or near the very top layers of the Earth's crust was only a small part of all the life on Earth. Plants, people, possums, porpoises. These were only a small fraction of the much larger biological history of the planet. In the depths of the Earth's crust is a second realm, a hot bacterial biosphere that has a greater mass than that of all the creatures living on the surface of Earth and swimming in the seas.

Most biologists would tell you that life is something that only existed at or close to the Earth's surface, powered by sunlight and requiring water and organic food sources to sustain itself. However, Smythe theorized that most living organisms actually reside at great depths within the Earth's crust at temperatures well above the boiling point of water, and we're surviving on the methane gas and oil that are created even further below the surface.

The world wouldn't learn if his theory was right or not until a couple of years later. After Smythe submitted his theory on the deep Earth biosphere for publication, a joint partnership between teams from the University of Oregon and John Hopkins University proved Dr. Smythe right once again. Bacteria were discovered thriving in volcanic vents near Baja, California, at temperatures well over 480 degrees Fahrenheit. Even more surprising, rare clams, crabs, fish, and giant tube worms were also discovered, not just surviving but thriving in a surreal, zero sunlight environment and metabolizing only inorganic substances.

Once Smythe had on a tuxedo that he despised wearing, he headed downstairs to the lobby and waited near the entrance for his ride. Soon the same limo that picked him up from Logan International and took him to his hotel pulled up in front of the lobby. He arrived at the university at 8:00 PM sharp on a typically damp, chilly evening in New England. The driver parked the car, walked around, and swung open the rear door.

As Smythe stepped out of the cozy, warm comfort of the limo, he was pleasantly surprised to be greeted by none other than Fred Ressner, who was equally surprised to see Smythe at such an event.

"Thomas, it's great to see you again, my friend. Congratulations, by the way, on your incredible triumph in Sweden."

Seeing his old friend Ressner, Smythe was finally able to let his guard down, and the emotions began pouring out. With a tear in his eye, he approached Ressner, and once he was close enough, he gave him an out-of-character hug that caught Ressner completely off guard. Fred knew something was off, but before he could ask what was wrong, Smythe began.

"Thank you so much, Fred; it's great to see a real friend here, if you know what I mean. The Swedish experiment just goes to show that even an old broken clock is right twice a day." Although he was often outwardly outspoken, Smythe possessed a unique trait that Dr. Fred admired but could never grasp the contradiction.

On occasion, he had an almost unattractive mannerism that allowed him to come across as a cold, careless man. At other times he had an astonishing ability to persuade people, even his critics, to sooner than later accept the genius of his theories. He was a lot like their mutual friend Francis Crick in that way. Fred always thought that Smythe would have been one hell of a salesman if science hadn't got in the way.

When asked about his newest project, Dr. Smythe was much more restrained than usual. Fred simply thought that his old friend was jet-lagged from the long flight to America.

When Smythe finally began to loosen up and share his thoughts on a subterranean biosphere, he said, "Fred, if my theory is right, it could explain where some of the biomarkers we find in oil are coming from. It would also prove that abiogenic oil is actually feeding a biosphere deep within the Earth."

Without giving Fred time to respond, Smythe then said something that rocked Dr. Ressner. "But Fred, it's important I warn you that moving forward, we must be keenly aware of just who is following our work. Be aware, I mean, be careful. More importantly, be diligent in taking necessary precautions; it might just save your life. It didn't save Cricks."

"What the hell are you talking about, Tom? What do you mean by that? Did something happen to Francis?"

In an instant, Fred became both concerned and confused by his friend's cryptic comment. He had never heard Smythe speak in this way, and the words coming from his mouth triggered a feeling of unease that left Ressner queasy and lightheaded. He caught himself swaying on his feet, beads of sweat already beginning to form on his forehead.

His thoughts immediately went to Crick's strange behavior at his party. Smythe didn't want to say anymore, fearing it would ruin their evening, but Fred pressed him hard to
elaborate.

"Are you saying Crick is dead? Thomas, Please!"

"Yes, dammit, Francis was murdered. Murdered in his
own home, the very home we recently saw him at."

Fred took a moment to think, but then, like anyone who
knew Crick well, his initial reaction to Crick's death was that
he was most likely killed by a jealous boyfriend or husband.

"The authorities said someone had intentionally caused
a natural gas explosion to cover the murder, Fred."

"But Tom, unfortunately, gas explosions aren't uncommon. You know how old those damn underground pipes are
around the outskirts of London. Hell, even in America, it
seems there is a massive failure a couple of times a year,
blowing up homes that hurt or even kill people. Perhaps it
really was an accident?"

"Fred, do you recall the night of the party when Francis told us that he was about to completely renovate his kitchen? He wanted it to be ready to impress his guests before his next event. You know Crick would never have his guests eat catered food. He always hired top chefs to come to his home and prepare the food fresh in his own kitchen on the day of the party. He insisted on it and wanted to have the best appliance money could buy, top-of-the-line stuff all the way, Fred. He even paid extra and had them professionally installed by one of the oldest and highest-rated contracting companies in the city.

"Fred, what I'm about to tell you will be unpleasant and quite difficult to hear, but the explosion was massive. It leveled most of the estate. Only small bits of the body were recovered. The largest part, his head, was found outside in his own barbeque grill. It had been charred black and was still smoking when the fire and rescue finally arrived.

"Fred, the coroner, found deep cuts on the vertebrae of his charred neck. The weapon that was used was found about a hundred yards away, blown from the house by the explosion. It appears Francis's head was hacked off with one of his own meat cleavers while he was still alive. His mansion was then blown to bits along with the rest of his body. This was clearly a signal Fred."

Smyth continued speaking in a soft, serious tone, "Fred, they are watching closer than you know."

"I know Tom, but who? Exactly who is watching us? And why?"

Smyth refused to say any more as he continued to scan the giant ballroom where the fundraiser was being held. As he did, he noticed two men who appeared to be out of place, standing in corners, not talking, not eating, not drinking. They were standing motionless like statues in a museum just watching the crowd.

"Oh, Shit!"

"What, Fred? What is it?"

"The man standing to the left near the bar. Do you see him?"

"Yes, what about him?"

"He was at Crick's party, Tom."

"How can you be sure? Are you absolutely positive?"

"I'm more than positive. Do you remember that strange-looking tattoo on the side of his neck I pointed out to you? That is the same man we had tried to confront before he disappeared off of the back balcony. Smythe had now become even paler than the Englishman usual was."

"I'm sorry, Fred, but I just can't say anymore right now. Let's just somehow get through tonight and plan on meeting somewhere as soon as we can to figure this out. I will tell you everything I know then, but for now, I think it would be best for us not to be seen together for the rest of the evening. And Fred, stay in sight of people, try not to go anywhere alone."

The two men quickly checked to make sure their contact information was up to date before going their separate ways, promising to email or talk on the phone as soon as possible.

Unfortunately, that never happened. Just a couple of days after the fundraiser, Ressner was stunned when he read about a horrific story that came across the morning online news feed on his phone. A dismembered body had been found in New Bedford, just about 60 miles south of Boston.

Regrettably, today in America, random, brutal acts of violence are not uncommon. So much so that they rarely make the national news. Before Fred could even read the name of the victim, an uneasy feeling came over him while he read the headline.

"Remains of dismembered man discovered in New Bedford."

Up until the murder of a prestigious international scientist, the small fishing town located about an hour southeast of Boston was best known as the setting for the great novel Moby Dick.

Ressner continued to read as the story went on about a group of teenagers that had broken into an old, abandoned whale blubber refinery for a night of drinking and tagging the dingy walls of the dilapidated building with graffiti. Needing to reach higher up to complete their artwork, a couple of kids spotted some old rusty 55-gallon drums close by and thought they would try moving one of them closer to the wall to stand on.

As they tried to tip the drum on its edge to roll it closer to the wall, the weight became too much for them to handle. When the drum quickly slipped from their hands and tipped over, the lid popped off as it smashed down hard onto the concrete floor, spilling out and forming a large puddle.

Standing in the darkness, the only light they had was coming from half a dozen cell phone lights. The kids couldn't immediately make out what they were looking at as they began slowly walking closer to examine the spill, using their phones to navigate through the dark. Being careful not to step in the thick, black liquid, the strange yet familiar shape of the object that lay in front of them became clearer. Several yelled in horror when they could finally make out the shape of the arm that had spilled out onto the dirty, cold floor along with about 40 gallons of jet-black crude oil.

The body had been cut up into six pieces and stuffed into six separate 55-gallon drums. The exact number of drums that Thomas Smythe had extracted from the granite during his tests in Sweden. It was a gruesome murder, the type usually done by someone either extremely sick, very evil, or someone who wanted to send a message.

Fred then thought it may have been the work of someone who fitted all three descriptions. Smythe had become victim number two. Like Captain Ahab from Moby Dick, whoever the men were who killed his friend were obsessed with killing but for even more sinister reasons than revenge. They killed more for pleasure than for the money.

Struggling to fight back his emotions that were moving from shock to anger, then sorrow, Fred suddenly recalled the final words of his friend.

"They are watching. Crick was murdered. Be aware."

At first, Fred was skeptical of his friend's warning, but now after reading the gruesome details of Smythe's murder, he was now convinced that someone was sending a very clear, very loud message. He also thought of the very real possibility that he could be the next one to receive it.

Then, like turning on a light switch, Fred recalled the POP...POP...POP noise he had heard back on campus in Boulder and the black SUV that sped away just afterward.

Oh my God, he thought to himself as he realized he may have been the first intended target of whoever these people were that had brutally murdered his two friends.

As a man of science, Fred was accustomed to dealing with facts and logic, not senseless acts of violence. After the murder of his colleagues, Fred felt a sense of relief that after either a premonition, instinct, or subconsciously he knew that the popping noises he heard were gunshots that came from the black SUV he saw. Whatever the reason, he felt thankful for the random but wise warning to his interns to watch their own backs.

The fear Fred was feeling after the murder of Crick and Smythe was understandable. It was the kind of intense, life-changing experience that few people would have ever had to deal with. Fred couldn't eat or sleep much for days while trying to figure out what to do next. He then realized that he had to make a difficult decision; he had to call Kim. He simply couldn't take the chance of going back to school and risk being either kidnapped or killed, and he couldn't return to his cabin and wait for his turn for execution.

Since he and Kim had not been together for several years, he felt it was the safest place he could go while he prepared some kind of plan. His exodus back to the mountains of Colorado was not only to flee from danger and hide but was also a way he could buy some time. He promised himself to see to it that his two closest friends did not die in vain.

CHAPTER 10

Kim didn't typically take calls if she didn't recognize the caller ID on her cell phone. She had put her number on The National Do Not Call Registry more times than she could count, but somehow, they just kept on calling. On the rare occasion when a telephone salesman's call did make it through to her, she took pleasure in leading them along for as long as possible before not so politely telling them to fuck off. Not to mention a few bad dates that had led to some part-time stalking by a couple of infatuated weirdos, she was tired of changing her number. But for some odd, unexplainable reason, something felt different this time. As if a voice inside compelled her to answer the phone. Like not wanting to look at a bad car accident as you drive by, but you do anyway, or maybe it was just her intuition; for whatever reason, she just had to answer that phone.

Kim had been on her own for several years now and had become stronger and more independent. But just in case she was right, and it was indeed another salesperson or creep calling, she came out with both barrels blazing. After she swiped the ANSWER button on her phone, she quickly said, "Listen, if this is a perv I dated once, get it through your stupid skull that I'm just not into you, and if this is a sales call, I already have everything I need, so please remove me from...."

"Kim, it's Fred." Having no time to waste on small talk, Fred quickly explained to her that he was calling from a landline in a gas station just in case his own phone was being monitored. Fred was clueless when it came to electronics but had seen enough spy movies to know that if someone wanted to, they could easily listen in on his cell phone conversations.

"What are you talking about, monitored silly? Did you lose your cell, Fred?"

"Kim, please listen carefully. I don't have much time."

"You're scaring me, Fred. What's wrong? Is it the kids? Are you OK? What's going on!"

"The kids are fine, Kim, but I might not be. I need to come over after class this afternoon. Is that OK? It's important, Kim."

She knew there was no way in hell Fred would ever want to come over unless something wasn't seriously wrong.

"Yes, of course, it is. I will be here all afternoon after my morning hike with Fritz. Just come on in when you get here; you know where the key is."

After ending his call to Kim, Fred realized that his decision and the risk he was about to take by going to class for one last lecture was simply too stupid for someone supposedly so smart to do. All he could think at the moment was, "damn you, mom and dad," as the lessons they instilled in him as a kid about dedication, hard work, and loyalty might just end up getting him killed. It just wasn't in his nature to simply blow off the kids and not show up without giving his class one final lesson and some type of explanation why he might not ever be coming back.

It was 9:55 am, and since Fred had wisely chosen not to park in his designated parking spot, he had just 5 minutes to race across campus to the Swenson building where the earth sciences classes were held. He was 3 minutes late for class when he busted through the back door, startling most of his students who were already seated and waiting.

Breathing hard, sweating, and visibly shaking, Fred could hardly contain the look of panic in his eyes. He tucked his shirt in, smoothed his hair back with his hands, and took a few deep breaths. While the class watched in bewilderment, one student asked, "Dr. Ressner, is everything OK?"

The pause wasn't intentional, as Fred was having difficulty finding the right words as he forced himself to speak. "Uh...oh, yeah. Yes, I'm OK, I'm fine. Thank you. Please, forgive me, but today's lecture will be quite full, so please feel free to record this as I won't have time to stop and answer any questions. Also, this might be my final lecture."

"What's going on, Dr. Ressner? Are you sure you're OK?"

The distress on Fred's face was transferring to his class, and he hated that he was doing this to the kids. "Yes, everything is fine. I am just taking a little time off to handle a personal matter. Please, let's just get started, shall we?"

Since the late 1960s, virtually every kid that has attended a public school not just in America but around the world had been taught to believe an incredibly simplistic and still unproven theory called biogenic oil formation. After being cast out by his peers and ridiculed around the world, Dr. Fred's priority in life was to change this culture while he still had time. He continued his final lecture.

"Biogenic simply means that oil was created within a relatively small window of time from decaying animal and plant matter. The theory continues to be taught to this day despite the fact the total volume of known oil reserves today not only continues to grow, but it far outweighs the total mass of every living organism in the history of the planet."

"How many of you have ever heard of another false theory called Peak Oil?" As Fred suspected, not a single hand went up as he proceeded with his grand finally. "In 1930, the demand for oil in the United States to power factories, heat homes, and fuel planes, trains, and automobiles hovered around 2 million barrels a day, and the national average cost for regular unleaded gasoline at that time was about 20 cents a gallon. Twenty years later, in the early 1950s, the amount of oil consumed in the United States had nearly quadrupled to just under 8 million barrels a day; however, the cost of regular unleaded gasoline only increased to an average of about 27 cents per gallon. How is this possible? Many of you have learned in ECON 101 about price and demand, right? The higher the demand, the higher the cost. Although oil companies had seen an impressive increase in sales due to the rise in manufacturing and transportation, their profit margins remained stagnant or had even shrunk once labor costs, refining, distribution, and later advertising and marketing were factored in."

This was a highly competitive time in the oil industry. Oil companies engaged marketing agencies to come up with new and innovative ways to draw more customers away from their competitors' gas pumps and to their own. Probably among the most widely implemented idea was the full-service gas stations that featured windshield washing, oil level checks, tire inflating, and gas pumping. Full-service gas stations popped up all over the country so that the American consumer could remain in the comfort of their enormous, gas-chugging couches on wheels. They could now spend just a few pennies more per gallon to be treated like royalty. Eventually, though, the full-service concept was realized to be flawed. More and more full-service stations chose not to provide the services. Instead, they simply sold their gas for less money. The full-service concept that was initially designed to increase sales had backfired on the oil companies as it further ate into their profit. These stations have been gone for decades, and most of you have probably never even heard of them until now."

The companies that held onto the full-service station concept began to see even further erosion of already thin profit margins, and American oil companies were not happy. Something more had to be done to generate higher profits. The solution to the problem came in 1956 from an American geophysicist named Dr. Marion King Hubbert."

Working for the Shell Oil Company in Houston, Hubbert coined the phrase "Peak Oil," a term that is still referred to today. Hubbert was a well-respected and award-winning scientist. Soon, his theory would play a significant role in global oil production for decades to come. Peak Oil is a concept that has altered the wealth of most countries around the world to this day. Hubbert believed in the biogenic theory of oil, and that meant since oil was produced from rotting plant and animal matter, one day, the world would simply run out of it. Adopting the Peak Oil theory allowed countries with large oil reserves to control the market by increasing prices or decreasing output at will. This has been a tremendous policy for oil companies but a disastrous one for consumers."

The belief in a quantitative, finite supply of oil has led to countless wars, coups, and global supply chain shortages as a result of the fear of running out of fuel. Today, some feel that Hubbert's high-level position at Shell and the theory of Peak Oil he promoted were no coincidence. The possibility that he was simply a pawn of the giant oil companies used to convince the world of a looming crisis was real. Peak Oil would mean that those countries without oil or had a limited supply would have to embark on extreme measures to ensure their supply of oil remained uninterrupted."

The simplistic theory of Peak Oil also meant that one day production output would eventually fall behind increasing global demand, and the world would literally run out of oil. Although it took time for the plan to catch on, Peak Oil finally took root within the industry. By the early 1970s, oil companies finally realized the tremendous leverage it gave them. In part, the scheme helped send America into the 1970s oil crisis and ensuing panic that lingered for decades."

From October 1973 to March 1974, an oil embargo that slashed production was enacted by the OPEC countries. While, in reality, the production cut was planned and carried out as retaliation against the United States for supplying arms to Israel, it was described in the media as a global geopolitical issue and blamed squarely on the oil-producing counties of the Middle East that participated in it. While they were outwardly condemned for the action, the ability of the Oil Producing and Exporting Countries, OPEC, to use oil as a bargaining chip had precisely created the desired effect the oil companies secretly wanted to achieve from the Peak Oil theory. During the six-month embargo, the cost of a barrel of oil increased by over 300%, and oil profits skyrocketed."

In 1980, the US, in conjunction with the 13 countries that make up the OPEC oil cartel, finally agreed that a more accurate system of reporting oil reserves was needed in order to maintain some degree of uniformity. They needed a way to prevent another embargo like the one of 1973 that caused gas prices to quadruple, created long lines at gas stations, rationing, and panic across the country. America could not stand for this, as it nearly crippled the country."

In 1980, the first global estimate of total crude oil reserves was presented. To create a formula, several factors were combined, such as the geology of the area and the location and pressure of the untapped oil reserves. Geophysicists and petroleum engineers from around the world were finally able to agree and come together to create what they believed to be a reliable method of calculating reserves."

Based on their calculations, the first total global oil reserves reported in 1980 came in at approximately 650 billion barrels. Despite a significant increase in consumption over the last 40 plus years, particularly the insatiable appetite for fossil fuel in China, the estimated worldwide oil reserves in 2022 now stand at nearly 2.9 trillion barrels. Yes, you heard that right! During a 40-year period of incredible growth in the transportation and manufacturing industries, oil reserves have quadrupled from 650 billion barrels to 2.9 trillion barrels, according to Engineering and Technology Magazine! Not possible, right?"

Coincidentally, during this same period of time, from 1980 to 2022, the global population has nearly doubled from around 4 billion in 1980 to just under 8 billion people today. When considering this massive surge in population combined with increased travel and factory output, there should have been a major drain on the world oil supply. However, annual global oil reserve reports during this time have consistently increased nearly every single year with only 4 or 5 exceptions. You heard that right again. Over a 40-year period of incredible global growth in both population and manufacturing, oil reserves have increased 4-fold! Again, not possible!"

But according to an article published in Science magazine, there is an explanation. They wrote that "there is a bounty of precursors in place within the earth for it to continue to produce massive amounts of oil naturally."

Obviously, the proponents of Peak Oil are those that have the most to gain - and also the most to lose - from these inventory calculations. This is why they continue to stick to their tired, old argument that the growth in total oil reserves is due to new technologies such as fracking and diagonal drilling. This is despite the fact that shale oil represents only a very small percentage of the total amount of oil in reserves. Also, the oil obtained by diagonal drilling has already been included in these calculations."

Kids, the problem is these estimates only factor in oil that can be reasonably extracted and is relatively close to the surface. They do not account for the oil that is being created deep within the earth that eventually seeps to the surface. That is the real cause for the estimates to continue to increase nearly every year."

As I mentioned, Hubbert had based his Peak Oil theory on the notion that there was a finite amount of oil within the earth's mantle/crust interface. After all, there were only so many plants and animals that ever existed to create all the hydrocarbons on the planet, right? Because of this limited supply of plant and animal matter, there was also a limited supply of the byproduct, oil. Amazingly, for some reason, Hubbert did not factor oil migration into his theory, even though he was a staunch advocate of the concept. He had written that there was no doubt that oil could move from regions much deeper in the mantle and up through cracks and fissures within the earth to layers higher up in the crust!"

There are many documented cases that have proven the fallacy of Peak Oil. In 1971, an enormous reservoir of high-quality oil was discovered in an area found about 80 miles off of the coast of Louisiana, 170 miles southwest of New Orleans. Mostly submerged underwater like a massive earthen iceberg, Eugene Island rises up nearly 11,000 feet from the floor of the Gulf of Mexico. By 1972, over half a dozen deep water rigs were pumping over 95,000 barrels per day of crude oil from the reserve. The Wall Street Journal reported that by the late 1980s, output of one of the main producing wells known as rig 300 had declined to less than 4,000 barrels per day. At which point it was considered to be pumped out. It was dry. Kaput! It was costing more to operate the well than they were extracting from it."

But then, in 1990, something interesting happened. Production had soared back to up to 16,000 barrels a day, and the reserves, which had been estimated to be around 60 million barrels in the early 1970s, were recalculated to be holding more than 400 million barrels of oil, according to the US Department of Energy."

Stranger still is that the geological age of the oil is younger! The laboratory tests that we talked about earlier proved the new oil is significantly younger than the oil that was pumped in the 1970s. Seismic recordings of the area revealed the presence of a deep fault at the base of Eugene Island. The fault, or fissure, was allowing a much deeper reservoir to gush up in a river of oil and replenish the reservoir that had been nearly pumped dry."

Another case of oil reservoir replenishment occurred in the icy waters off the Alaskan Coast at the Cook Inlet oil fields that were discovered in late 1960. This site is considered to be the birthplace of commercial oil production and one of the first major oil boom discoveries in the state. The discovery reassured the United States government of its investment in the purchase of the land that led eventually to granting Alaska statehood in 1959."

Soon after the Cook Inlet discovery, 14 platforms were erected in the years between 1964 and 1968, producing 225,000 barrels of crude a day until its peak in 1970. But by the early 2000s, the amount of crude being extracted had dropped so low, about 10,000 barrels a day, that most of the platforms were shuttered. Some were slated for decommission, and one company was set to move into bankruptcy as it was no longer generating the revenue from the reserve to be self-sufficient. Once again, the big players pulled up stakes and moved on to more lucrative reserves."

By 2011, younger, smaller, and more aggressive oil exploration companies swooped in and brought the abandoned wells back online, increasing production from less than 10,000 barrels a day to over 16,000 barrels a day and growing. A far cry from its heyday of the 1960s, but incredibly, today's estimates of the reserves in the Cook Inlet fields that were originally set at approximately 231 million barrels in the late 1960s were revised to be over 1.3 billion barrels. An increase of a factor of 6! Not possible, right?"

Then we have the expansive oil fields in Uzbekistan and the Middle East that have also experienced this phenomenon. A mind-boggling amount of oil has been extracted by the Middle East countries over the last 50 years. Despite that, the known reserves have more than tripled since estimates began in 1980. At that time, ARAMCO, the Saudi Arabian oil company, reported that there were at most 248 billion barrels of oil. In a recent report by BP, British Petroleum, today, the estimated amount is somewhere around 830 billion barrels. Guys, creating the amount of oil reserves we have across the world would require a larger pile of dead fish, dinosaurs, and fermenting prehistoric plants than has ever existed!"

As I mentioned, oil reserves only count oil that "could be reasonably extracted." This means within several thousand feet beneath the surface, in the crust. The deepest well ever drilled on dry land is the Bertha Rogers Number 1 in

Oklahoma. In 1972, the Lone Star Company had drilled down 31,000 feet in search of hydrocarbons. Before they reached deep enough to tap the natural gas, the drill hit a pocket of molten sulfur and destroyed it before reaching the vast natural gas reserves below. You see, hydrocarbons begin at incredible depths within the earth, then migrate to the surface."

On yet another side note, some people mistakenly believe the Z-44 Chayvo in Russia is the deepest well at over 49,000 feet deep, but most of that is diagonal or horizontal, not vertical. An interesting fact, another well also located in Russia called the Kola Super Deep Borehole, though not technically an oil well, was also over 40,000 feet in total length. It was abandoned in 1992 because scientists actually believed they heard screams of the damned souls of hell! Creepy, right!"

As I was saying, the theory of abiogenic oil means that it is created at levels of well beneath 5,000 feet and closer to 20,000 feet deep or more. To date, only a handful of wells have ever been able to reach a true vertical depth of 7,000 feet."

So, class, to quickly summarize, in 1980, there were estimated to be approximately 650 billion barrels of oil on the planet. Today, the estimate is over 2.9 TRILLION barrels and could rise to as high as 4.8 trillion by 2050, according to Engineering and Technology magazine!"

It had become common for Fred to run over his allotted 55 minutes. Today, he went on for over 70 minutes, yet his lecture was so compelling that nobody in the class seemed to notice, or if they did, they didn't seem to mind.

CHAPTER 11

The students gathered their belongings and stood up to leave while they talked and speculated with one another about Ressner's odd behavior. Olympic sprinter Usain Bolt would have been impressed as Fred raced toward the back door exit when his lecture was over. Once he had made it outside the building, he stopped and slowly scanned the area looking for anyone who appeared out of place. Surrounded by hundreds of young students, they would be easy to spot. The jog back to his truck seemed to last an eternity as Fred kept his head on a swivel.

When he had finally made his way back safely to his truck, another spy movie popped into his head. *Dammit, what if there's a bomb attached to the ignition switch,* he pondered to himself. Fred was now both mentally and physically exhausted. Not so much from his hectic lecture or his mad dash to class and then back to his truck. It was mostly from the enormous stress of the last month. He had arrived at the point that he just didn't care anymore.

"Screw it, he said to himself. "When you gotta go, you gotta go. But if they blow up my beautiful dream truck, I will be so pissed!"

With the keys still in his jacket pocket, all he had to do was push the start button, but his trembling right hand was shaking so much that he was having a tough time just doing that. Fred closed his eyes tightly enough that a small tear formed in the corner of his eye and rolled down his face.

As he sat and waited on the courage to come to him, he thought about his life and how much he missed his wife and kids. Before anyone could see him sitting alone and crying in his truck, he said a quick prayer, tightened his sphincter, and began to count down from 3 before hitting the start button. 3…2…1…ignition! The purr of the 8 finely tuned cylinders and Ode To Joy that was still blasting in his CD player had never sounded better than it did at that moment. For the moment, he was safe.

The drive to Kim's house would take about 30 minutes, giving Fred plenty of time to wrap his mind around the situation he was in. Talking out loud to himself had now become a habit as he asked himself, "Am I being paranoid? Am I going crazy? Should I go to the police?" Navigating through campus and onto Colorado Boulevard through town, and onto Highway 36, Fred drove for miles without realizing it.

He had drifted into a deep state of thought and had no memory of the last 20 minutes. It was seemingly as if his truck had driven itself.

One of the main selling points that led Kim to buy her house was its privacy. Hidden by the Colorado hills and dense evergreens and no numbers on the mailbox, it was even difficult for Amazon delivery drivers to find her unmarked driveway. As he pulled up to her house, Fred thought it would be a perfect place to lie low.

No sooner than he opened the door of his truck, Kim and her terrifying black German shepherd Fritz had just finished their hike and were there to welcome him. One with a smile and one with a gnarl. The combination of the enormous weight Fred was carrying along with the fact the two hadn't seen each other since Christmas with the kids, Kim thought the hug he gave her would nearly crack her spine. "Oh my, it's good to see you too, Fred. Let's grab your things and get inside. It looks like rain."

The house looked beautiful compared to Fred's minimalist mancave in the woods. Shockingly, his cabin only looked slightly better than the uni-bombers shack and only had a few pictures of their kids and fish scattered around the walls inside. Kim, on the other hand, had exceptional taste and worked as a successful home decorator around Boulder. Before Fred could even set his things down, Kim began to ask him questions, and rightfully so. She still loved Fred and noticed that his nervous behavior was a drastic contrast to his normal calm and casual personality. It was upsetting to her.

"Kim, I promise I will tell you everything, but right now, I'm exhausted. Can I please take a quick shower and a power nap first? I will fill you in on everything as soon as I get some rest."

Not having a good night's sleep in almost a week, the nap ended up lasting over 3 hours, and Fred woke up to Kim in the kitchen cooking dinner.

"Perfect timing. Are you hungry?" Fred hadn't been able to eat much in days, but now that he felt somewhat safe, he devoured the fresh trout Kim made. It was his favorite meal, even if he hadn't caught it himself. After dinner, they cleaned up the kitchen slop together while Fred explained the entire situation to her. He even included sharing with her the gruesome details of the recent murder of his two closest friends.

Waiting on her reaction, Fred was surprised that she wasn't shocked to hear the news. "Fred honey, you've been poking the bear for years. I am sorry about your friends, but you know who you have been pushing. My God, Fred, you have written books and magazine articles about them. Did you not think they might retaliate someday?" Her sermon was affecting Fred's digestion and was frustrating him, even though he knew she was right.

Not wanting to ruin the evening by getting too deep into the weeds, Fred simply apologized, agreed with her, and then asked for a drink. "Kim, do you have any Stranahans around?"

"You know I do, silly. I'll pour us both a double."

When she joined him in the living room with the drinks, Fred had already started a warm, cozy fire for them to relax, but what she had said to him after the diner was still festering. Before he could fully let his guard down and relax, he could no longer hold back the urge to get everything off his chest. If only to finally explain to her what had sent him on his course of self-destruction for the last 15 years.

"Kim, since the 1980s, we have all been manipulated, the entire world, by a cancer. It is a tumor that has festered, mutated, and has now grown out of control. It is now spreading faster than ever and has considerable momentum, particularly among the younger generations. They all want to save the planet, but the planet doesn't need saving. We do.

Do you remember in the late 1970s, there was a major national magazine that published an article on "The Coming Ice Age?"

"Yeah, wow, I think I do remember that!"

"That story was filled with facts and compelling evidence. Christ, it even featured a picture on the front cover of the earth covered in ice to really get our attention. But somehow, for reasons I believe are politically motivated, just a few short years later, the narrative had shifted from global cooling to global warming."

"But Fred, today, who really cares if oil is a renewable resource? A lot of people believe that humans are causing global warming. They just want fossil fuels to go away. Why is this mission still so important to you, baby?"

"For the principle, I suppose. And because it's all a lie. Not long ago, there was a powerful politician extraordinarily close to the president of the United States who profited tens of millions of dollars by writing a book and narrating a documentary on our impending doom. He was swimming in money while condemning others for their selfish lifestyles that he claimed were causing global warming. To this day, that man continues to fly around the world in private jets and is chauffeured in the back of bulletproof, gas-chugging SUVs. Public documents even showed him to have electric bills of over $30,000 a year at his 20-room mansion. Of course, with a pool house. Now tell me, if this man genuinely liked the taste of the crap he was forcing down our throats, would he not try to change his own extravagant lifestyle? Instead, he went out and bought yet another oceanfront mansion in California!

Then we have the billionaire boy wonder, who is so concerned about the environment that he started an electric car company while at the same time sending his rockets into space. Each one spewing out nearly 2700 tons of carbon dioxide with each take-off. To date, this guy's company has launched over 143 rockets, so at 2700 tons of CO_2 per launch, his company has churned out over 386 thousand TONS of CO_2 into our atmosphere. He and his elitist buddies now want to launch over 1,000 rockets a year which, at that pace, will put out a whopping.... wait for it.... grand total of two million seven hundred thousand TONS of added CO_2 into our atmosphere. In comparison, today's highly efficient combustion engine automobiles put out only about four and a half tons a year."

"I can go on all night with more samples of the Kool-Aid we have all been given to drink, but I'd rather not."

"I'd rather you not either. I believe in you, Fred. I've always believed in you. I just have a heavy heart that your passion has not only fractured our lives but now has put you in serious danger."

Fred was reading Kim loud and clear. With better agility than he had walked on a cracked sidewalk a few days earlier, he quickly changed the subject to something lighter. They began sharing old stories of better times they had with the kids and their college days. The conversation went on for hours, and an orange sun began to set behind the still snow-capped mountains.

Even before the bottle was empty, the feelings for each other were beginning to creep back up. Not sure if Kim was feeling the same way, Fred offered to sleep in the spare bedroom, but to his pleasant surprise, Kim firmly shot down the idea. If there was one thing Kim and Fred were compatible in, it was their sex life, but as they headed to her bedroom, his cell phone rang. "Dammit," he mumbled to himself, but at least this would give time for the little blue pill to kick in.

Just over a week had gone by since the brutal killing of his friend Thomas Smythe. Fred had thought about the murders of both his friends, Crick and Smythe, about every minute of the day since then. Now, whenever his cell phone rang, his anxiety level would immediately spike. Kim pleaded with Fred not to take the call, fearing it would ruin their evening. Like Kim, Fred typically didn't take calls into the evening either. Especially ones with numbers he didn't recognize. He tried to ease her mind by explaining that it might be one of the interns he was mentoring or possibly the university checking in on him after his meltdown in class earlier. Fred assured her he would cut it short and then asked her to be ready when he was done.

Before choosing to live his life in hiding at Kim's, Fred had been very careful over the last few days. Particularly where he went and who he talked to. He wasn't sure how the caller got his phone number, but he was determined to stay calm and cool so he wouldn't upset Kim. But it was hard to keep his promise while his insides were beginning to turn into knots. As he reached for his phone, the memories of the events of the last two weeks flashed in his mind, terrifying him as his phone continued to ring.

He could tell the bourbon had affected his coordination as he fumbled for his cell. Finally getting a grasp on it, Fred quickly tried to stop the ring tone that his intern Jason had programmed for him. Although it's a classic song, this just didn't seem like an appropriate time to hear "I Like Big Butts."

"Hello......Who is this...? Hello...? Is there anyone there...?" Rob Wiley froze, then nearly hung up the phone, thinking that Dr. Ressner might think he was some kind of a quack. Wiley immediately regretted his decision to make the call, but it was too late to turn back now. Damn caller ID, he thought to himself.

"Uh, yes, hello, is this Dr. Ressner? Dr. Fred Ressner?"

Fred answered the phone and heard the voice of an enthusiastic but perhaps overly confident young man who described himself as an industry upcomer seeking Fred's advice. He was beyond suspicious.

"Yes, this is Fred Ressner. Can I help you?"

"Yes, you don't know me, sir, but my name is Rob Wiley. I am the senior engineer for the Permian Oil Company."

"I've never heard it," said Fred.

"Yes, sir, it's a very small, family-owned outfit." Wiley proceeded by profusely apologizing for the late call, which helped to soften up an already very tired and moderately buzzed Dr. Fred.

"OK, so what do you want, Wiley, and how did you get this number?"

Like Ressner trying not to lose a huge trout on his line, Wiley first began by explaining to him that the contact information for "Dr. Fred Ressner" is listed in the campus directory. Wiley then went on to say what a fan he was of Fred's work. He even mentioned that he had read a couple of his publications.

Still skeptical, Fred tested Wiley and said, "Haha, no shit. Name one!"

"Well, sir, I felt that the article you submitted to World Energy magazine was not only intriguing but groundbreaking as well."

"Come on, son, are you screwing with me! Groundbreaking, my ass. Not only was that NOT groundbreaking, but it was also borderline plagiarism.

Fred was a social drinker only and not particularly good at it. Wiley could hear the hostility in Fred's voice coming across the phone. Now that his favorite Colorado whiskey had kicked in, Fred was beginning to lose control of his thoughts and his tongue. He unloaded on the random stranger who had the unfortunate timing of calling when he did. The combination of fatigue, alcohol, the murder of his friends, and the battle that he had fought for so long was making it hard for Fred to hold back his emotions.

"Son, that article was based on research from over a hundred years ago. The recent data was mine, yes, but I rode the coat tails of some great research scientists to get that article published."

Not aware of Fred's mental condition, Wiley was taken aback by the raw directness of the conversation and was now feeling even more certain that he had made a huge mistake by calling. He was trying desperately to politely end the call when out of nowhere, a moment of clarity came over Fred. As if the whisky had somehow evaporated from his bloodstream, he asked Wiley, "So, exactly where is this miracle oil located, Mr. Wiley."

"How did you know I discovered oil?"

"That's easy; why else would you be calling me?"

When Wiley answered the question, Fred's head began to clear even further as he sat up in his chair.

"Where did you say? In west Texas near the Permian!"

"Yes, that's right. Does that surprise you?"

"Well, no. On the contrary, I have been waiting for this day for quite some time."

"Why is that, Dr.?"

"Mr. Wiley, Can I call you Rob? You read my article, and you're a petroleum engineer and geologist, correct? Then you should already know the answer to your own question unless, of course, your career path has been motivated more by money like the rest of your generation rather than putting in the time and effort to research how things really work."

Wiley had envisioned the conversation going much differently, and while he could never be considered a delicate snowflake, he became slightly agitated by Fred's comment. After all, Wiley did extensive research on the oil he discovered, and he certainly didn't have to reach out for help. Fred was confrontational and had snapped at Wiley like an older, seasoned teacher losing his patience in class. But still, Wiley felt humbled as he realized that within 3 minutes, Fred had accurately described what Wiley's career was really all about. To make as much money as he could and as fast as he could. Rob Wiley had a childhood that had made him somewhat disconnected and immune to harsh criticism, especially criticism coming from a drunk. This was simply an exercise in patience as Wiley calmly waited for Fred to cool down.

He was still trying to turn the conversation around as he thought that working together could be mutually beneficial. Wiley felt forming a partnership could be the best thing for both men. He fought the urge to snap back or defend himself as that would only further agitate probably one of the only men in the country that would believe him. More importantly, the only man that could help him. Since Wiley didn't drink alcohol, he had no choice but to swallow his pride and allow Fred to continue with his pissing contest.

"Listen, son. I'm tired, I'm old, and I've had a long day. Let's just cut through the crap and tell me exactly what data you have from the Permian. But before you do, just know that the odds of not only finding abiogenic oil but also having the resources and presence of mind to even have it analyzed is nearly an impossible mission. A shot in the dark to say the least. If you are as familiar with my work as you say you are, then you know that I have spent the good part of 25 years trying to prove the theory. Out of hundreds, maybe thousands of samples I have analyzed, I have only identified two proven cases of replenishment. And what do I have to show for it? A divorce, a strained relationship with my kids, and my friends murdered! I certainly would not want that to happen to you."

Wiley had suddenly found himself in the unusual position of actually feeling connected to another person. "I understand, Dr. Ressner, and I truly appreciate your concern. But I wouldn't have called if I didn't think we might be able to help one another. Please, sir, just take a look at the data. If you don't find anything here worth your time, I promise I will never bother you again. But if you do, I hope you consider coming down to Midland to see for yourself."

"OK, OK. Since you've been so persistent, I'll make a deal with you. If you email your data to me tonight, I will review it in the morning and get back to you as soon as I can."

Wiley was ecstatic. "Great. I will send you everything I have as soon as I hang up. Thank you, Dr. Ressner."

"Well, don't thank me now. I haven't done anything yet."

CHAPTER 12

Now 39 years old, Wiley had spent his entire childhood and teenage years helping on his family's west Texas farm. His father Rick had leased out over a dozen small but steadily producing derricks to a local oil company as a side hustle to his cattle business. Not much meat on longhorns, but as a 4th generation Texan, his father felt somehow compelled to raise them. Life for the Wiley family was good, but when Rob's mother was diagnosed with pancreatic cancer when he was just 14 years old, things quickly turned upside down for the little family of three. The only symptom Gina ever mentioned was an occasional stomachache and fatigue. This was a silent killer.

When after a few weeks, she began vomiting blood, Rick finally persuaded his young wife to see a doctor. "Just to rule out anything serious," he said. By the time she finally agreed to go, it was too late. Doctors drew blood to run tests, but it was the CT scan that quickly showed them that Gina was in the advanced stages of the disease.

The prognosis of just eight weeks to live was shocking. They left the hospital in disbelief and drove back home in sad, uncomfortable silence. Rick didn't know what to say. He was terrified to talk, fearing she might break down. He did the best that he could by simply pulling her close and holding her tight until they got back to the ranch.

Finally arriving back at the farm, none of them was able to sleep that night as the jolt of the diagnosis had evolved from denial to shock and, ultimately, fear and depression. The next morning, they all talked and prepared for what was about to come over the next few weeks.

An avid naturalist and believing that clean eating, herbs, and meditation could cure anything, Gina refused her doctor's advice. She knew that the aggressive treatment would have made her final days feeling even more lethargic and sick than she already was. Life at home became difficult during her brief illness, even on her good days. It was sometimes downright intolerable on her bad ones. The disease didn't only destroy Gina; it was devastating for both Rob and his father Rick as well. She chose to pass her last days with the same dignity she lived her life.

Toward the end, her final wish simply became pain management. The only medications Gina would use were morphine and the potent strain of Indica she harvested in her small hydroponic unit at home. She smiled, remembering the countless times when she and Rick would light up for recreational use. Now she was just thanking God for the gift that helped her sleep and manage the intense pain.

Like a lot of families, it seemed that mom was usually the glue that held everything together. For the Wiley family, Gina was the super glue. Losing her short battle at only 41 years old was devastating to Rob and his father.

Rick seemed to get through his days drifting along like a feather in the wind, not knowing which way he was going from one day to the next. He began drinking soon after, thinking it would ease his sadness, but it had the opposite effect. He never became physically abusive to Rob, but rather he became something just as hurtful and destructive to a young boy; he just didn't give a shit about anything anymore. Including his own son.

It was an awful place for a kid to be. Rob was trapped between hating the world for what had happened to his mother and trying to understand what his father had become. He felt as though now he had lost both parents. Incredibly emotionally strong for a young kid, Rob spent his last few years of high school suppressing his sorrow. He chose to drown his depression by studying harder rather than abusing alcohol and weed like most of his classmates. He had turned into a loner and saw academics as his only real chance to make it out of their small town that held so little opportunity.

During his senior year, graduation loomed. Rob became more and more torn in the final weeks before he had to leave his dad on the ranch to go off to college. Although he had dreaded the day and tried to prepare well in advance, he still wasn't fully aware of the difficulty of his decision. On the one hand, he felt guilty leaving his dad alone on the farm. He even considered giving up his scholarships to stay closer to home and attend community college so he could be there to help his father. On the other hand, he was excited and anxious to finally be getting on with his own life. His teenage years had made Rob mentally strong, and he was proud of what he had overcome in the last 3 years. He decided that now was his time to make his mark on the world as he headed off to a school that had one of the top chemistry departments in the country.

Wiley excelled in college and worked towards dual degrees in petroleum engineering and chemistry from the University of Oklahoma. Like Ressner, he had spent countless nights in the school library, sacrificing relationships and missing out on far too many tailgating parties at Sooner football games. The only social life he really had was hanging out with his equally driven, equally introverted roommate Nate Jones.

At first glance, a brainy petroleum engineer wouldn't have much in common with a journalism major, and the two

roomies had both wondered why the university had randomly placed them together. After orientation for the new incoming students, the two finally met while moving their things
into their tiny dorm room. Although neither of them said
much, after sizing each other up, their initial thought after
the meeting was that this was going to be a brutally long and
awkward freshman year.

Sitting and talking the first few days together in the tiny
dorm room, Wiley and Nate soon formed an instant connection due to something that they had in common. They were
both introvert-loners in high school. They would both set
their alarm clocks to go off at 7 am every school morning,
then go their separate ways for the day. Wiley headed to the
chemistry lab while Nate, depending on what day it was,
went either to the Gaylord building of journalism or the
Price building for his business classes.

Nate usually finished studying early in the evening, just
after dinner. An hour or two later, when Wiley would usually
make it back to their dorm, they would hang out in the claustrophobic 10-foot by 12-foot dorm room to watch TV, play
video games and talk. Even though the talking part would
usually only be 15 or 20 minutes, catching up on each other's day and staying connected became an important ritual
for both of them.

As the weeks rolled by, turning into months and the months to semesters, the roomies continued with their usual routine. They showed that they genuinely cared for one another as they would listen, motivate, and encourage each other. Even when they were too tired, had to cram for an exam, or just didn't want to talk. Nate learned that Wiley had an even tougher time as a teenager than he did, and he did his best to inspire Rob, even if it was only for a few brief minutes each evening. The two remained best friends and roommates for their entire four years at Oklahoma, and by senior year they had become as close as a lot of brothers, maybe even closer.

Most of us think we really know our friends and family, but we don't always know the real, dark, ugly secrets or the beautiful dreams they have hidden inside. But for these two, it was different. They knew each other, as well as they knew themselves, so well that they could even finish each other's leftovers without getting into a fight. An extremely impressive undertaking for young college men who could consume massive amounts of calories and would guard their food like it was their last meal.

Nate also came from a family that believed and taught him that nothing worthwhile is gained without hard work. He was a quiet kid instilled with the morals and principles he inherited from his lower-middle-class parents. Like Wiley,

Nate didn't spend too much time chasing girls either. The fact was, neither had any "game" getting girls, as they often joked. As much as they each wanted to be part of the popular cool kids, neither one really had much interest in putting in the effort of being more social or joining a fraternity.

Nate didn't realize it as a kid, but his parents didn't just have a tough time making ends meet; they were downright poor. They had married young thanks to a shotgun wedding, still a thing in the remote part of the Louisiana Cajun swamps where his parents had grown up. Since neither of them was able to go off to college, they had vowed to do whatever it took to see that their only son did. His parents tried to save as much as they could, but ultimately, they had to borrow thousands of dollars in student loans to fulfill their vow to their only son. Aware of this incredible sacrifice, Nate remained vigilant and was determined to somehow, someday, pay back every cent they had borrowed for him.

Even though they both had different reasons, keeping their focus and staying on track was a shared vision for the two roommates. The university's random selection that paired them together eventually felt like divine intervention to both of them.

Internships for journalism majors are incredibly scarce. Nearly as impossible to achieve as winning the lottery or not growing old. As Nate grew out of his awkward late teenage years and into his early 20s, he discovered that he had a hidden talent. He had developed a remarkable natural ability to seemingly morph into a totally different person when he was in front of the camera or the classroom. He could even lose his Cajun accent when he needed to. He was reluctant, but Wiley encouraged him to send a demo video to a small local television station where he hoped to get an interview.

"What have you got to lose, bro? All they can do is not call you back," Rob said. Turning on the charm like a light switch and cheesing his bleached smile when the bright light of the camera came on, Nate tried his best to impress the management team at the station. When they saw the video of Nate anchoring a news desk and reporting a fictitious event, the small station reached out for him to come in for a tryout in person. With Rob's encouragement, Nate won the coveted intern position he desperately needed.

His career path in media and journalism had started years earlier, though, when he worked in the AV club at his high school in exchange for free school lunches. Until now, Nate was always a behind-the-scenes kind of guy. He loved running the cameras, editing footage, and splicing clips to create incredible videos. His high school would often show his work at assemblies, rallies, and basketball pregame and halftime shows to pump up the crowd. Inside though, he had always secretly wished that he had the nerve to go in front of the camera just once and show what he was capable of.

Six years later, with Rob's support, years of practicing reading scripts in front of mirrors, therapy sessions for his anxiety, and the help of some potent CBD gummies, Nate had finally broken out of his shell. He was now excelling in front of the camera and on his way to fulfilling his dream.

After Nate graduated from Oklahoma, Wiley followed his career as he went on to larger and more prestigious jobs. He eventually made it all the way to his goal as the evening news anchor at KDAA television in Dallas. A leading station in a major market, Nate had done it! He was able to keep his promise to his parents and, in no time at all, was able to pay back every cent of tuition they had unselfishly given him.

Rob and Nate stayed in touch through social media, texting, and video calling. Twice a year, they would meet over long weekends to hike in the beautiful hill country of Texas just west of Austin. A location about halfway between the two.

After graduating with honors, Wiley also landed an enormously lucrative job at one of the largest refineries in the country near Galveston, TX. After spending 17 grueling years in a room packed full of high-powered computers and no windows, Wiley was finally making the kind of money he had dreamed of. Sacrificing so much of his high school and college years had paid off. He had spent years as a kid working on the family farm, countless hours of late-night studying, and now under tremendous pressure from the demanding responsibilities of his job. Wiley was beginning to feel burned out. Despite the exceptionally high paychecks, it began to feel to him that he had worked his entire life with nothing to show for it except for a lot of zeroes in his bank account.

Even so, when the job offer came in from a small drilling company located close to his father's West Texas farm, his first reaction was to laugh, say, "Do you know who I am," and hang up on the recruiter.

Although the longer the headhunter talked, the more Wiley realized that while this would be a significant cut in pay, it just might also be a good time to make a drastic lifestyle change. The luxury of having no family or social life allowed him to leave his job with a large nest egg approaching seven figures. Not bad for anyone, especially someone still in their 30s. He also thought about his dad and how he wanted nothing more than to reunite with the only family he had left.

Rob accepted the job and soon found the simple day-to-day tasks to be invigorating. The days of production quotas and the relentless "What have you done for me today" questions from his bosses were soon left far behind. He felt as though he could finally breathe again. The laid-back owners he now worked for provided him with nearly as much nurturing vitality as the fresh west Texas air. Leaving the massive refinery behind proved to be worth every penny he gave up as the years of stress began melting away.

Wiley was now in charge of monitoring just over 100 relatively old injection oil rigs. Called injection rigs because the low volume of oil remaining at the bottom of the wells required water to be pumped at high pressure down into them. The technique would keep the old dying wells alive as long as possible to suck every cent of oil from the bottom of them. Once determined to be dry, wells are typically capped and abandoned, although sometimes they aren't even capped as the well-owners consider that an unnecessary expense.

Unlike most of the oil saturated Permian basin, the area near Midland where Wiley had begun his new job was considered to be a dead field. Most of the larger oil companies had long moved on only to set up operations in the lucrative mega fields where oil strikes were nearly guaranteed. In Texas, Alaska, and around the world, crumbs were often left behind for the smaller "mom and pop" wildcatters. Just like the one that hired Wiley as a senior engineer. These companies generally had very little overhead and required only a modest profit to earn a decent living.

One of Wiley's favorite tasks at his new job was taking the company truck out in the morning for routine field inspections. It gave him the alone time he missed while at the refinery while he was cramped up in a claustrophobic control room with a dozen other engineers and technicians. One morning a few days before calling Dr. Fred, Wiley was making his usual rounds out in the field. His job was to make reports of any broken down pumps, repair fence lines, calibrate pressure gauges, and chase away wild animals that had strayed onto the property. It was on this morning when Wiley noticed something strange going on with the gauges. Downhole electronic monitoring devices that Rob had installed on all the wells to monitor pressure were showing a significant buildup. At first, Wiley thought that they were probably just malfunctioning, but when he recorded nearly a dozen gauges with increased pressure, he knew it could only mean one thing. The wells were refilling.

He had heard about the phenomena in college, but it had never been formally taught in any class. He remembered one professor in particular joking about some fool named Reasoner or Ressner or something like that. Apparently, the man had, in effect, canceled his own career when he went off the deep end and began working on proving a crazy theory called abiogenic creation. "New oil can be created like some kind of voodoo magic," his professor joked.

"Ressner probably thinks he can turn water to wine too," his professor went on. At the time, Wiley considered this to be more thought-provoking than funny or crazy, but he never gave it another thought until now. The purity of the oil is typically determined in a laboratory using a very expensive, extremely complicated piece of equipment called a gas chromatograph. An expensive, very intricate, and very sophisticated piece of machinery that uses pure gases such as nitrogen or helium to separate out various elements from a small sample of oil. Since the molecules of elements vary in size, the point at which they separate out of the gas can then provide a type of fingerprint and prove exactly what was present in the oil. Of course, the owners of the small company Wiley now worked for couldn't afford or see the need for such a high-tech piece of equipment. As a result, Wiley decided to reach out directly to his Alma Mater, the University of Oklahoma, for help.

It had been over 15 years since Rob had last spoken to any of his Professors. Fortunately, while he was in school, he had made such a positive impression that they not only remembered him but gladly agreed to help analyze his samples.

Once explaining to the university that several of his aging, dried-up wells had recently begun to refill, they insisted that Rob bring them his samples so they could run the tests for him at no charge. Partly because he was a successful and

esteemed alumnus, but also as part of their community out-
reach program. Not to mention they would love the publicity
they would receive having their name associated with one of
the most significant oil discoveries of the Permian basin in
decades. An eager and excited Wiley was there the next day.

After analyzing the chromatograph data from the new
oil and comparing it with samples taken decades earlier, Wiley could hardly believe his eyes as he reviewed the results.
He could immediately see that the oil was not the same. Not
even close. The new oil had virtually none of the organic res-
idues. The biomarkers that most oils contain, including the
samples taken from the same wells years earlier, were missing. While trying to process the information, Wiley slumped
in his chair and rubbed his tired eyes in disbelief. He then
once again recalled the ridicule and insulting remarks his
former college professor had made about Ressner and abiogenic oil while he tried to figure out what he should do with
the information.

When Wiley shared the data with the owners and explained what was happening, they were in total disbelief.
When he then said they would be putting eight wells back
online, there was more excitement in the office than at a Texas rodeo. They had absolutely no hesitation giving credit to
Wiley for finding a way to extract more oil from the dying
wells even though he really had nothing to do with it. The

celebration began as they poured shots of tequila and patted each other on the back. They also toasted for agreeing to bring Wiley in at a much higher salary than they had offered dozens of other applicants who applied for the job.

As more shots were poured, the owners continued on and relentlessly pressed Wiley to spill the beans about how he did it. "Son, most of those wells were pumped out back in the 80s. Hell, most of 'em were nearly dead when we bought into this dried-up piece of dirt. We were just hoping to make a decent living without workin' too hard!"

Wiley was still confused with the findings himself and was trying to process the information. He knew they wouldn't understand the report, so he made up some crazy stories about magic beans and purple unicorns that gave the owners a good laugh. Rob wasn't a drinker, but the owners insisted. After a few shots of tequila, he reluctantly accepted their thanks and then quickly headed out the door for the day while he could still drive.

Once he was back home, Wiley went straight to his laptop and fired it up. He clicked on the DuckDuckGo icon and typed "Fred Ressner" into the search bar. He scrolled past about a dozen unrelated listings, including a realtor, a salesperson, and one a murderer, all named Fred Ressner.

Wiley then typed, "Dr. Fred Ressner geologist." The information that popped up was overwhelming and impressive, although about half of it was negative. On the second page of listings, he came across an old article submitted years earlier from the World Energy Trade Publication written by Dr. Fred K Ressner. The very same article that launched the downward spiral of Dr. Fred's career.

CHAPTER 13

Fred didn't get out of bed until nearly 9 am the following morning. He wasn't generally a late sleeper, but with the combination of the drinks, the fire, talking with Kim, and the four and a half minutes of incredible sex, he found himself waking up in a much better mood than he had been in years. Kim was already out of bed, and as Fred staggered to the kitchen, he found her note, "Gone for a hike with Fritz, be back by 10 am."

Fred then saw the bottled water and banana sitting by the note. After so many years, she still remembered his morning routine of chugging a bottle of water to rehydrate and eating an apple or banana rather than coffee to get his neurons firing.

Fred began to slowly emerge from a mild hangover while catching up on the morning news. Traveling around the country for years, he began to despise watching local TV news as he believed it was nothing more than scripted propaganda mixed in with a few depressing reports of shootings, muggings, and traffic jams. In fact, at one point in his career,

Fred was traveling so often that he began to notice a bizarre trend. After the standard first five minutes of junk news that the broadcasts typically begin with, they would always seem to then jump right into the exact same national story of the day with comments and editorials that were nearly identical from city to city.

On one recent trip, he began his day with the morning news in Miami, and when he arrived at his hotel in New York and caught the evening news, it was like Déjà vu. The exact same story and the exact same commentary as they talked about COVID. There was never really any useful information; even the weather forecasts were only right about half the time. Fred didn't really consider it news. It was only background noise while he prepared for his day.

"Finally annoyed with it," Fred stopped what he was doing and yelled back at the television.

"WHY DON'T YOU DAMN PARROTS REPORT SOME REAL NEWS FOR ONCE."

When he was done venting, he peeked out the bedroom door to make sure Kim wasn't in the house. Anyone who knew Fred Ressner knew that yelling at the television was way out of character. Like most Americans the media treated as sheep, Fred had woke up to the propaganda years ago and was fed up with all the false narratives. He always said, "Science is not about popularity; it is about facts."

While waiting on Kim to return from her hike, he remembered his conversation with Wiley before he had gone to bed. Opening his laptop to catch up on his emails, Fred was pleasantly surprised to see that Wiley had made good on his promise and had already sent the information they had talked about. The PDF attachment wasn't long, about nine pages that included lab reports, maps, geological data, and even a detailed history of the region. Although Fred was well aware of the enormous oil reserves around the Permian Basin of southwest Texas, what he was about to read instantly grabbed his attention. Not at all like the meteorologist still blabbering in the background.

It didn't take Ressner long to study the information Wiley had sent, but this wasn't about quantity; it was about the quality of the data. Within those nine pages, what Rob sent was more than enough information to convince Fred to change his upcoming travel plans to Titusville. After taking a few minutes to process the report, he decided to call Wiley back.

"OK, Mr. Wiley. You have my attention. But first, I want to apologize if I was rude last night; things have been, well...." Rob interrupted Fred before he could finish his apology. He was so ecstatic hearing that the world-renowned Dr. Fred Ressner was actually coming to work with him that he quickly cut him off.

"No, sir, no apology needed. We've all been there, Dr. Fred. We all have a cross to bear. I certainly have mine. I'm just relieved and extremely thankful that you found in my report that we might actually have a major discovery down here."

"Well, Rob, I tell you what, let's just take this one step at a time, my friend. After all, I've been deep down so many rabbit holes by now I'm beginning to hate the sight of carrots. And frankly, at this point in my life, I've learned not to set goals. That way, I'm never disappointed with failure, but I'm always happy as a hog in shit with my successes. Sorry, that was probably too many animal references. I'm going to load up my gear now and head that way as soon as I can get out of here."

"Great! I'm looking forward to meeting you in person, Dr. What time do you think you'll be getting in the area?"

"It will be late. I'm going to try to leave by noon, which would make my ETA around 10:00 pm or so."

Kim was still out on her morning hike, so Fred still had a couple of minutes to make a quick zoom call with his interns before she returned. Sharing the details of the newly discovered abiogenic oil in Texas, Fred told them that his plans had changed and he was no longer going to Titusville.

"Please, be safe, Dr. Fred," Sangen said.

"Yeah, man, keep us posted, doc," Jason added while Henry remained quiet. Fred then began loading up his truck for the 10-hour drive from Boulder to Midland.

After Fred gave Wiley his commitment to come to Texas and work with him on his research, Wiley decided to further explore the man and his career in greater depth. If anything, Wiley was usually very well prepared. Using the DuckDuckGo browser again, he scrolled through about five pages and read the links to even more that detailed Fred's amazing career. But there was one web page in particular that stood out most of all because it had clearly connected Ressner to Thomas Smythe and Francis Crick.

As he continued to read on about the horrific, unsolved murders of the two men, Wiley was beginning to grasp the unsettling dynamics of the situation that he now had the unfortunate fate of becoming a part of. Fred and his colleagues knew they were deep in a no-fly zone for years as they continued to publish claims of fraud, market manipulation, bribery, extortion, and insider trading. Allegations of serious white-collar crimes committed by dozens of the highest-ranking politicians and board members of some of the largest corporations in the world. Reading this, Wiley was simply bewildered. Despite being considered great thinkers, mathematicians, and scientists, none of these men had even had the slightest inclination or concern about the slippery road they had been traveling for so long. Or the potential repercussions it could bring them until it was too late.

Wiley was now fully aware that Ressner was in deep trouble. But he didn't know that the murders of his colleagues had terrified Fred to the point that he had just left everything behind, even his beloved fly fishing gear, had abandoned his home and his job at the university. He was now hiding out at his ex-wife's home and was living like a fugitive. When Wiley connected the dots between the murders and Dr. Fred, his thoughts naturally gravitated to his own safety. Wiley knew there was a high probability that these people, whoever they were, were tracking Ressner by his cellphone, and Fred would have no way of knowing until it was too late. He somehow had to get a message to Fred, but how? Ressner was at his ex-wife's house and would be leaving soon to make the grueling 10-hour drive to Texas.

Wiley had no choice but to take a chance and warn him of the danger they were all in, but after their divorce, Kim had gone back to her family name, and after an hour of searching in vain, Rob failed to find her contact information online. This was a woman who knew how to live off the grid so effectively that nobody except for a couple of stalkers she had briefly dated after the divorce could easily find her. Wiley had given up.

The only idea he could come up with was risky, but he hoped it could save all three of them. It was now past 10 am, and he was running out of time. Rob had no choice but to call Fred on his cell and explain his plan. This time, it was Wiley who was controlling the conversation.

"Hey Rob, did you forget something?"

"Dr., we don't have much time; please listen to me very carefully. You must leave immediately and, for God's sake, bring Kim with you. DO NOT PACK. DO NOT LEAVE KIM. Go back to the campus and call me back as soon as you can get to a secure landline. Dr., this is extremely important. Put both of your cellphones in the microwave and destroy them NOW."

"Oh my God. I just told my group of interns I was going to Texas." "Fred, there's nothing you can do about that now; just get out of the house as fast as you can."

The panic in Wiley's voice was now quite obvious to Fred, so he followed the instructions without asking another question.

Kim had just returned home from her hike with Fritz and had not even had a chance to say good morning before Fred asked for her phone. Tilting her head and thinking what a strange request it was, she reluctantly handed Fred her cellphone. As he sat her down and began to explain Wiley's instructions, he placed both phones in the microwave and hit the popcorn button. Kim's eyes bugged out, and her jaw nearly hit the kitchen table as she put her hand to her forehead and shrieked.

"NO! Dammit, Fred, have you lost your mind? What the hell are you doing?" But the more Fred talked, the angrier Kim became.

"Fred! What the fuck have you done? You led murderers to my home? I can't leave here. I won't leave here; I have nowhere else to go."

"Kim, I know that saying I'm sorry won't cut it right now and probably never will. Honestly, I would be quite upset too. But if we don't get the hell out of here right now, neither of us will ever have to worry about buying another cell phone again."

An intense glare then came across her face. She revealed to Fred that she understood there were no options, but she was angry. She either had to go with him or face whatever evil might be coming.

"Fine. But Fritz is coming with us, no questions, got it!"

Fred's belongings, just a couple of suitcases he had quickly packed for his trip to Titusville before going to Kim's, were already out in his truck. He already had one foot out the door when Kim insisted on at least filling a backpack. She quickly grabbed a change of clothes, underwear, socks, her toothbrush, and some makeup before they scrambled to the truck Fred had parked close to the house.

Finally ready, they rushed out of the front door and ran to the truck. They had only made it about 15 feet from the house when Fritz stopped dead in his tracks, slowly lowered his head, and stared dead ahead at a large evergreen tree on the side of the gravel driveway. The thick, coarse hair running down the center of the dog's back stood straight up, and he let out a deep, unnerving growl. Fritz was warning Fred and Kim that they were not alone. Kim had lived by herself in the woods for so long that she wisely felt that for her protection, it would be a good idea to have Fritz professionally trained by a police officer who had recently retired from the local canine unit. Until that moment, she wasn't even sure if Fritz had paid any attention at all to his training.

The killer slowly slithered out from behind the large Colorado blue spruce and into view. Fritz could instinctively sense the bad intentions. The assassin began to reach into his jacket to pull out his 40 Caliber Ruger, already loaded and the safety off, but Fritz didn't hesitate. He was only able to get a single shot off that missed everything as Fritz lunged on top of him and took him to the ground. Weighing about 80 pounds, Fritz wasn't a massive dog, but the 6-year-old German shepherd had a bite pressure of about 280 pounds per square inch, and he used every ounce of it.

Shepherds don't have the most powerful bite, but it was more than enough to do considerable damage as he was taught to clamp on and shake and tear the flesh like a shark attacking. Fritz had been well trained and latched firmly onto the right hand, the one holding the weapon. He continued to shake it violently from side to side like it was one of his play toys. In seconds, the man's hand was nearly torn off, only attached by two of the six tendons that connect that hand to the wrist. Flailing and pulling his arm away from Fritz, the blood was squirting and spattering in all directions. The gun flew from his dangling hand and landed directly at Kim's feet.

The former special forces operator who came to kill them was well trained. Somehow, he was able to block the intense pain while using his weight advantage and strength, wrestled Fritz to the ground, lay on top of him, and put him into a choke hold using just one arm. Fritz whimpered and squirmed as he fought to escape from under the man's weight, but after a few agonizing seconds that seemed to last forever to Kim, Fritz was asleep.

With the guard dog now neutralized, the man quickly removed his belt and tightly cinched it around his forearm to prevent himself from bleeding out before he could finish his job. His badly mangled hand was dangling and still spurting blood as he began staggering toward Kim and Fred, but it was too late. Kim had already picked up the weapon that was flung during the struggle and was lying at her feet. She didn't hesitate to use it as she fired two shots. The first bullet struck the killer in his voice box. He clutched his throat tightly with his left hand as the blood began to gargle in his throat and drooled down the corners of his mouth, staining his teeth bloody red. The second shot struck him just beneath his left eye, blowing out the back of his head. Blood, chunks of brain, bone, and hair flew back into the blue spruce that he had been hiding behind.

"Oh my God, FRITZY! Please God, no, no, no. Fred and Kim were both horrified at what had just happened. He knelt down, trying to console her as she lay down next to Fritz, but she pushed him away. Not only was Fritz her protector, but Kim had raised him from a puppy. After six years of being together in the isolated mountain house, she and the kids considered him as family. Fritz never asked for anything and was always happy to see her when she would come back home from work or running errands. Kim was now overcome with emotion at the thought of losing him. She refused to let Fred comfort her, blaming him for what had happened, shrugging him away again.

"Kim, I am so sorry. I understand you are hating me right now, but we have got to go. There may be others coming if this guy doesn't check in with whoever sent him here."

Kim quickly wiped away her tears, then slowly stood up, looked at Fred, and slapped him. "You asshole, what were you thinking coming here!"

Unfortunately, what was done couldn't be undone. Despite his good intentions, Kim was right. Fred had brought the fight to his own doorstep, and the opponent was undefeated. While doing so, he had not just succeeded in waking up a monstrous beast, but he had also pissed it off. The enormous reach of its tentacles had no boundaries, like some kind of global medusa. It could find and destroy anyone, anywhere, at any time.

Once they were both in the truck, Fred slowly began to head down the long driveway to the main road, but as he glanced in his rear-view mirror, something caught his eye. Fritz was still lying where they had left him, but he was beginning to slowly lift up his head. He was alive! Kim began to cry again, this time in joy. Fred backed the truck up, opened the backdoor, and laid Fritz in the back seat. Pulling onto the road, they were both still in a mild state of shock, thinking of what had just happened, and Kim was still mad as hell. They headed down Highway 36 south toward the campus, neither of them saying a word the entire way there.

Fred was eager to get as far out of town as fast as possible, but he intentionally drove the speed limit to avoid getting stopped by the police. He thought that whoever had sent the hitman could be listening to police scanners hoping to hear that the killer had completed his task. Upon arriving at his lab, Fred called Wiley as he had directed, "Rob, it's Fred."

"Fred, are you OK?"

"Yes, thanks to you, we are. I guess you were right; they must have tracked my cell phone and found me at Kim's house. We had to kill a man Rob. Kim is upset, to say the least."

"I would be too; that's awful. OK, Fred, have you ever heard of Proton mail?"

"No, never. What is it?"

"Proton is an encrypted email service created by the scientists at the CERN particle accelerator. That's the lab on the border of Switzerland where the guys developed the internet back in 1989."

"Yes, I'm familiar with CERN."

"Fred, I need you to go to the Proton website and register a new account... like now! When you're done, get the hell out of town ASAP. When you get about an hour or so away from Midland, send me an email using your new Proton account. It will be encrypted and can't be traced, but do not divulge your location or any other information. Just send a blank email; I will be watching out for it and will give you further directions once I receive it."

"OK, I got it. I'm doing it right now. Rob, thank you again. You saved three lives today."

"Three?"

"Yes, Kim's dog was nearly killed by the man who came to kill us. He's OK, though."

Once Fred had the new account set up, he closed the laptop he kept in the lab and bolted out of the building and back to the truck. Watching from a library window just across the greenway from the earth sciences building, Henry saw Fred running from the building and sprang into action. Fred had no way of knowing, but the dean who had Henry placed on his team was paying him three hundred dollars a week to spy on Fred and report on everything he was doing back to him. Once Fred was out of sight, Henry went straight to the lab and used the same laptop to send his final email.

"NOT GOING TO TITUSVILLE. GOING TO MID-LAND, TX ARRIVING TONIGHT."

CHAPTER 14

People often say that hard times breed tough men while easy times breed soft men. Compared to countries around the world, most would agree that Americans have become comfortably complacent over the decades with notoriously short memories and swim in our own waters, as shallow as they may be. We want our favorite football team to cover the spread, we want nice new cars and cheap gas to go in them, and we want money and sex. Not necessarily in that order. When it comes to foreign policy matters, we want our politicians to be diplomatic. Though, if necessary, we want the most powerful military the world has ever seen to neutralize our problems.

In stark contrast, our counterparts around the world think in terms of generations and millennia rather than months on the calendar. Our own short-sightedness explains why most Americans, even those who feel that they at least have a rudimentary knowledge of energy production and climate change, would consider Francis Crick, Thomas Smythe, Fred Ressner, and now Rob Wiley to be nothing more than an eccentric bunch of conspiracy theorists.

However, none of these men were the typical beer-drinking, nacho-eating, instant gratification types a good part of the world considered Americans to be. These were well-educated men who, through fate, were unfortunate to now all have another thing in common. They had all been either canceled or killed. These were the men that knew that the foundation of the true creation of oil had been poured over four hundred years ago by Georgios Agricola and his abiogenic theory. They also realized there was nothing they could do to change anything.

But toward the end of his career, the more disrespected Ressner felt, the more motivated he became. As a decades-long student of the history of his field, Fred was also well aware of the countless wars fought, the quasi-dictator puppets, and paid-in-full politicians that had been put in place. Over the last hundred years, they seized control of entire countries either by force or pseudo-elections simply in order to hold onto the great wealth they had been lucky enough to have been provided simply as a result of their geographic location on the planet.

In the last century of the great industrial revolution, countless people died protecting the flow of oil and the flow of money. Dr. Fred now feared he could possibly and ironically become the latest casualty in a cycle he helped perpetuate while working for the monsters he helped to amass their incredible power and fortunes. Kim told Fred that he had brought the fight to his own doorstep, but that might have been exactly what he wanted.

He never let it show, but the truth that he, Crick, and Smythe had all failed was infuriating to him. But even though his friends were now dead, Fred couldn't stop the events that were unfolding even if he wanted to. Besides, he still couldn't get the thought out of his head of what would happen to the world economy if he finally found the smoking gun. Proof that the product being controlled by huge corporations, governments, and families of unimaginable wealth around the world was actually as natural and limitless as water.

In Scotland, in 1907, the birth of the modern-day oil cartel was born. Two men, Henri Deterring of the Netherlands, nicknamed the Napoleon of oil for his major oil discovery on the Indonesian island of Sumatra, joined forces with a wealthy shipping magnate from England named Marcus Samuels. The Samuels family had accumulated most of their massive wealth shipping seashells across the world. In a time before plastics were widely available, shells were often used to make buttons, jewelry, and small cups and dishes. Once the merger between Samuels and Deterring was complete, the company named Royal Dutch Shell was officially established.

The two companies had united to be better globally positioned to compete with Rockefellers Standard Oil of America and the Rothschild brothers, who held massive oil reserves in Russia. After several years of battling for supremacy and control of world oil markets, negotiations would eventually take place between Royal Dutch Shell, Walter Teagle, on behalf of Rockefeller of Standard Oil, and Sir John Cadman of British Petroleum. Eventually, four more oil companies would be invited, including Anglo-Iranian Oil, Gulf Oil, Texaco, and another branch of Standard Oil called Exxon.

This group was given the name The Seven Sisters by Enrico Mattie, who was the head of the Italian state oil company in the 1950s. The title, based on the seven daughters of Atlas in Greek mythology, described the daughters of Atlas becoming stars in the sky to protect them from their enemies. Up until 1973, this powerful monopoly of massive conglomerates controlled an astonishing 85% of not only the global oil supply, but also its price.

Following the 1973 oil crisis, the United States government took what amounted to a figurehead position in the control of production, supply, and pricing of crude oil around the world. However, the original monopoly of the Seven Sisters still exists to this day with the addition of other major players, including OPEC, China, Russia, Venezuela, and Mexico. This group continues to hold regular public meetings in which the media is openly encouraged to attend. These frequent, glorified press conferences are scheduled to announce updated production levels as well as peak oil reserves forecasts that are nearly always either wrong or constantly later adjusted.

Within this massive, bastardized conglomeration also exists a much smaller but much more sinister faction that meets every month. The day and location of the meeting are only disclosed to its members days in advance in order to protect the security and identity of the group. This group is known as Argos. A name also derived from ancient Greek mythology, Argos was the son of Zeus. Believed to have been all-seeing and covered with 100 Eyes, the 100 members of the Argos group are the true puppet masters. Their monthly gatherings are held in order to set the real global production volumes, current global reserves, and the pricing of crude oil. The Argos conference is held to ensure that the enormous appetite of the insatiable beast, as hungry for wealth and power as a starving lion is for meat, is satisfied.

Unlike the circus shows that are routinely held in public for the media, Argos is a closed-door gathering usually held at one of the enormous private estates of the wealthiest men in the world. Due to the religious or cultural beliefs of several of its members, Argos consists of men only, but it remains a diverse collection of blue blood from around the world who unite for a common interest.

The world has struggled for thousands of years with war, famine, viruses, political unrest, and scandals, including worldwide pedophile rings. These issues are considered to be petty problems of the average person, but they are by no means meaningless to the Argos group.

In reality, many of these challenges are designed, created, and intentionally unleashed upon the blissfully unaware population around the world by the group not just as a game, but also to distract the masses of blind sheep while creating even greater opportunities to accumulate more power and wealth. In the dark, parasite-filled underbelly of the ultra-wealthy, where not many people ever see, fortunes and empires are made during good times, but they are considerably more prosperous during events of man-made disasters. The greater the catastrophe, the wealthier they become. In a recent article published by the BBC, just 1% of the world population controls about 99% of the world's wealth.

The Argos group was assembled and created with the purpose to be forever alive and prosperous, never to fall like the greatest empires of the past. Even with today's 24/7/365 global media coverage and online investigative groups such as VICE, most people around the world can't name a single member of Argos. These people are not the Gates or even Soros we routinely see on TV. Members of Argos were, for the most part, nameless.

For decades, they have successfully leveraged and diversified their grotesque wealth into pharmaceuticals, real estate, technology, and weapon contracts. But for many, the root of the disease grew from within the earth itself. Any attempt to expose one of the members was dealt with quickly, completely, and without conscience or concern of repercussion. Some consider this group to be the true "Illuminati."

Many members had inherited their vast fortunes, which meant that the Argos as a whole was not an inherently evil group. That title is delegated to another smaller, exceedingly exclusive unit within Argos that has no name. They are simply known as "The Insiders."

The responsibility of the insiders is to find and vet, sometimes for years but always without their knowledge, candidates who will do the dirty work required by the larger consortium. They typically target current and disgruntled former members of American Special Forces, MARCOS from India, Sayeret Matkal of Israel, and the British SAS. Recruited as the need arises, which is usually only when a current candidate is killed carrying out an order from the insiders. These were men that had once sworn oaths to their countries to "dare to win," "free the oppressed," and "be the few, the fearless."

Now, they were no longer the protagonists they were once thought to be. Using sophisticated algorithms, the Insiders used computer programs to scour the internet in search of keywords that would trigger potential members. The files of the candidates would nearly always contain some record of violations of a military code of conduct that usually had led to a dishonorable discharge, if not worse.

Although these men had vowed their oaths of commitment, in reality, they had joined their militaries for other reasons. There aren't many opportunities where you could legally kill a man, and even though wartime rules of engagement are still in place, even during times of combat these men clearly didn't like to follow those rules.

The Insiders would make contact with candidates, sometimes in prison, sometimes working private security jobs, and sometimes living a life of crime. Once they sank their teeth in, they made it extraordinarily clear to the candidate that refusing the lifetime membership into the small, elite group of problematic ex-patriots would not end well. Typically, without a trace. In another room, far from the other Argos members, The Insiders would be assembled for their orders. A group of 10 to 12 men, some well-seasoned and others middle-aged, would already be in their places making small talk until it was time for the candidates to be brought in and introduced.

The most recent gathering, like countless previous ones, was held in a room intentionally darkened by blackout curtains and dim lighting in order to mute the faces into faint blurs. The air quickly filled with smoke. Slowly dancing and twisting its way up from the cigars resembling small, swirling rivers of grey until it finally joined into a cloud lingering overhead. Swarovski crystal glasses held brown water, usually with no ice, in the wrinkled, boney hands of the elders.

The room was as enormous in size as it was grandeur, with 30-foot high ceilings and walls covered with the art of Picasso, Monet, and even some modern-day masters like Peter Doig and Artemisia Gentileschi. Two sprawling chandeliers and a massive stone fireplace were almost enough to take your eyes off of the exquisite, imported mahogany floor featuring an intricate inlay of African blackwood. One of the most expensive woods in the world.

The rich, warm atmosphere was further enhanced by the mellow aroma coming from an abundant collection of the finest American-made chromexcel leather chairs and couches that were hand massaged with leather honey every week by the staff. The smell of the leather could still be detected despite the cloud of smoke floating above. The beauty of the room was a surreal diversion and contradiction to the ugly, sinister plans about to be made here.

As soon as each candidate had introduced himself, The Insiders would ask each one-pointed, situational questions that would further aid in the selection process. Reviewing a man's resume was one thing, but hearing the tone of his voice, seeing the reaction on his face, and judging the speed and conviction of his answers held as much weight. Once the decision was made, the candidates that were not chosen were once again made perfectly clear that there was no place on earth they could hide and survive if they ever spoke of this group or of this meeting.

To emphasize the point, one was usually picked out at random and executed in front of the others. The body would be carried out by other current candidates and placed into a vat of sulfuric acid. Once the bones and teeth had dissolved and the body had turned into a gelatinous goo, it would later be dumped off at a local landfill or into the nearest river.

CHAPTER 15

After successfully escaping with his life and a small fortune from Skyview, Dry Hole Pete decided to leave California and return to his roots in West Texas. Retiring from the grueling work that had taken such a profound toll on his body and years of his life was an easy decision. Pete now had to wrestle with what to do with his newfound freedom, the fortune he earned at Skyview, and the remaining years of his life.

Scared of the stock market following the recession of 1920, Pete made the fortunate and the incredibly lucky decision to stay away from the stock market as the Great Depression would be coming soon. Pete carefully weighed his options, not at all like the gambling wildcatter of his youth. Learning how to drink while serving time in the Navy, Pete occasionally managed to invite an old friend from Tennessee, Mr. Jack Daniels, to join him in making his big life decisions. Although prohibition was in full lockdown mode across America in the 1920s, the whiskey was distributed by bootleggers for "medicinal purposes" at the time and was a rare but very appreciated treat. During one particularly heated financial consultation, Mr. Daniels urged Pete to buy a farm with his Skyview windfall.

Knowing absolutely nothing about farming, Pete had returned to his wildcat ways out of drunkenness and sheer boredom. The next day took most of his life savings as he invested $9,000, triple the annual income at the time, and purchased a 100-acre piece of dust and dirt near Midland near the Andrews County line. At just under $9 an acre, Pete was all set for his next big adventure.

He convinced himself and anyone that cared to ask that his decision to purchase such a desolate piece of land was mainly due to his roots in the area as well as his love for the natural beauty of the wide-open space, even though it happened to be flatter than a mirror. However, as Mr. Daniels had made it clear, the property also happened to be situated just outside one of the largest oil discoveries in America at the time, the new Permian oil basin.

Of course, as Dry Hole Pete's unfortunate streak of bad luck would have it, his new spread was completely cut off from the Permian Basin by a massive underground solid granite vein that stretched over a mile wide and several miles deep. A huge subterranean dam that ran southeast of Pete's property in a direct, diagonal line, all the way to the Rocky Mountains and began near Santa Fe 400 miles to the northwest. The underground barrier would ensure that no oil would ever make it from the Permian Basin to Pete's land.

Despite his obvious physical limitations and rough nature, Pete somehow managed to find a kind, loving prairie woman from Oklahoma to settle down with. Although he loved Kay, he soon found her meek and mild personality, combined with somewhat her limited conversational skills, left him quite frustrated and bored. During the cold, dark months cooped up in their tiny prairie shack. Pete often thought her personality had about as much excitement as the flat, tasteless griddle cakes she served with every meal.

Although they soon had twin boys to care for, Pete longed for the old days and comradery of his crew. He loved his boys, but the thrill of chasing oil provided him with his own purpose. A reason to get out of bed every day! As Pete's boredom grew by the day, the property was soon covered in dozens of pockmarks as he began randomly punching holes across the farm. Eventually, by some miracle and great persistence, he finally hit a moderately sized oil strike that provided a comfortable life for the family.

Sadly, Kay was not around to enjoy the riches for long as she lost her short battle with pneumonia during their ninth harsh winter on the farm when their twin boys were just eight years old. Although Pete had fallen out of love with Kay years before her death, losing her sent him into a deep depression as he began to neglect the boys in favor of drinking. Maybe from the booze, maybe because Pete was raised to be tough himself, or maybe knowing that if he didn't teach his boys to be resilient, they would never survive growing up poor in West Texas, it led to a hard childhood for both of them.

As they hit their teenage years, they both developed considerable wild streaks. There were countless encounters with the law for things that go hand in hand with young boys drinking. Fighting, vandalism, and disorderly conduct were considered minor nuisances at that time. The twins were usually held overnight, given a small fine and a big lecture, then sent straight back home to the ranch. When the boys were nearly 18, they finally lost their father to his long struggle with depression. He didn't use a gun, a rope, or a knife. Pete killed himself through years of heavy drinking that finally led to cirrhosis and a slow, painful death.

The boys were now on their own with little education and practically non-existent social skills. Somehow, despite not possessing good looks, charm, intelligence, or any other redeeming value to society, they both managed to meet a couple of local farm girls that had similar attributes. Both the girls, however, had even more baggage with their reputations in the town of being rather proud of their promiscuous ways. It wasn't long before the four of them would become six as both of the women had become pregnant, but there were rumors going around town that one of the girls was made pregnant by another man.

Agreeing to live together in the old farmhouse proved to be a mistake. It didn't take long to discover that four people and two colicky babies living under one small roof could be pretty damn unbearable. The living arrangements began well enough as all four were able to suppress their wilder impulses. Eventually, the friction created by people with such similar personality traits trapped in a one-thousand-square-foot house became pure torture.

One day while the boys were out mending fences at the back end of the property, the women decided to follow through on a plan they had talked about for months. They gathered the few possessions they had and left their husbands, the ranch, and their children behind for good. The twins had suddenly gone full circle, twice. From having a father, then being alone. To being married, to alone once again. But at least they still had their legacies. Their two young boys. The twins felt that the best possibility they had to survive and provide the boys with a good home was to stay on the farm and continue living the only way of life they knew.

So, they continued to earn enough money from oil to live comfortably, mainly since they both had exceptionally low expectations. After several years of declining production, the wells had finally dried up. When their sons were 17 and graduated high school, there was no hesitation as they imitated their own mothers and moved as far away from the ranch as they could.

With the income from oil now gone, a new plan was needed. With a little trial and a lot of errors, the local farmers' CO-OP helped them eventually achieve some modest success by phasing over the small farm from pumping oil to raising longhorn cattle. Seeming to finally gain some wisdom as they entered their 50s, they both agreed to keep the farm in the family once they were both dead and gone, even though neither had much contact with their sons.

They didn't have much money to spend on a lawyer, but a young local attorney, who was also a distant cousin, agreed to draw up the papers for a small fee. The farm would stay in the family as it was passed down to the firstborn son from generation to generation as long as the property taxes were paid and the boys could somehow be found.

CHAPTER 16

People often ask if it's worse being known as a has-been or a never-was. For Dry Hole Pete's great-great-grandson, Colton, the answer was simple. They both sucked. By the end of his sophomore season in high school, 13 division 1 colleges, including his beloved Texas Aggies, had already contacted the football quarterback phenom, his coaches, and his parents. An even greater accomplishment considering that sophomore year is the first year for incoming Midland students to attend high school as first-year students attended a nearby feeder school.

At 6'5" with a quick arm and even quicker mind, Colton was hyped as the next Peyton Manning. The hype spread like tumbleweed across the tiny Texas town that had seen five kids from Midland go on to play in the NFL, including Cedric Benson, the most recent draft pick from crosstown rival Lee High.

Unfortunately for Colton and his family, the dream of fortune and fame was turned off faster than the stadium lights one Friday night halfway through his senior season. On a quarterback option play, Colton had the choice of either throwing or keeping the football and running. He quickly scanned the Permian High School defense, and, in a split second, he opted to keep the football and run for the endzone. Sprinting out to the right then turning up field, he was at the 15-yard line, then the 10, then the 5. He could almost reach out and touch the endzone when, from his blind side, a violent collision came from his left. The defender dove at Colton, making the impact on his lower left leg at the exact moment he had planted it to dive into the endzone. The collision resulted in a horrific compound fracture that shattered Colton's lower leg.

Players on both teams yelled at the sideline for help when they heard the loud snapping of the bone. The atmosphere in the stadium instantly became somber, and the fans, who were cheering just seconds earlier, went silent as they heard Colton scream in agony. He was thrashing around on the artificial turf while pounding on the ground, trying to make the pain stop. Trainers ran to Colton and saw his tibia, the main load-bearing bone in the lower leg, jutting out of his sock like a broken tree branch. Colton drifted in and out of consciousness while a soft splint and ice were placed around the wound. An EMS team carefully loaded him onto a stretcher and then into a waiting ambulance. A mandatory safety protocol for football games. He didn't hear the solemn standing ovation from the crowd that had gathered mainly to see the phenom play.

The ambulance had Colton at the hospital in less than 10 minutes, but the surgery went on for hours as bone fragments were removed and his leg was reconstructed. After several weeks in a cast, Colton was finally able to walk again without using crutches, but had a noticeable limp. Although the physical pain was now a memory, the emotional pain and despair lingered well after his leg had healed. In this state, football is considered to be almost a sort of religion for young men. Still, just teenagers, those who played were treated differently from the non-athletes, particularly in the smaller rural towns. The thrill of competing, the pride, and of course, the insatiable desire to win at all costs were like fuel, especially to the small, isolated communities.

The recruiters stopped calling immediately after the injury. Colton eventually began to accept his fate and somehow remained thankful for what he had achieved. After a few years, the echo in his head from the roar of the crowd had finally faded away like turning the stadium lights off on Friday night. Colton settled down with his high school sweetheart, Paige, in their modestly furnished ranch home located about 4 miles northwest of Midland off Highway 349.

It was a beautiful, warm, and crisp summer morning in Texas when Colton nearly choked on his toothbrush as his wife's voice called out from the kitchen. His list of weekend honey-doos had just grown longer as Paige sweetly asked,

"Colton, honey, our water is sure tasting saltier every day. Will you have time to start on the new well today, or should I ask daddy to come to fix it?" Colton considered crawling back under the covers pretending not to hear her.

Since meeting in high school 10 years earlier, Paige's firm yet gentle power of persuasion had always been a good fit for Colton's carefree attitude. He had perfected the art of procrastination and was blessed with an uncanny ability to ignore the rattling water pipes, the salty taste of the water, and worse, the strong smell of oil coming out of them. But he loved Paige and wanted nothing more than to make her happy. A kiss on his stubbly cheek and an "I love you" later, she began her 10-minute commute to the Seven Eleven on the edge of town to begin her 7:00 am shift.

As Paige scattered dust from the rough, gravel driveway in her used 2015 Honda, Colton had a flashback to their glory days as Midland Bulldogs. Paige was a pretty girl but not the most beautiful in a school of nearly 3,000 students. A few of the cattier girls would call her "butter face" behind her back. Everything was good but her face. At 5'10" and ranging between 120 and 130 pounds depending on if it was volleyball season, she was tall and slender with thick black hair and green eyes. But it was her true and genuinely sweet personality that made her far more attractive to Colton than the future cougars that jealously teased her in high school.

Today, their lives seemed a million miles away from the embarrassingly irrelevant teenage dreams they planned right across the dusty town. Colton briefly wondered why she had stayed by his side after all the setbacks, then he quickly snapped out of his pre-coffee morning daze and suddenly felt a strong urge to express himself. First, making sure she was out of range, Colton bravely shouted his thoughts on the irony of the situation. "That damn ole well pumped just fine for my daddy for over 40 years, and now I'm the lucky S.O.B. who's gotta fix it?" He kept his eyes glued on the back of the Honda to make sure the taillights didn't come on.

The morning sky seemed to go on forever as it stretched out across the horizon of the flat land. Colton opened the warped back screen door, hobbled down the dried-out, creaky wooden steps, and stepped out onto the dry, cracked earth. Nobody would ever suspect that a rugged football player like Colton would ever notice or appreciate the beauty. The crisp, cloudless, early summer air that was only surpassed by the magnificent, vast Blue Bonnet field that spread out into the distance before him. As he yawned, stretched, and coughed on a deep cleansing breath, he took time to give thanks to God before going to work on the well. The ranch was located at an intersection on the edge of the Ogallala Aquifer. Also known as the High Plains Aquifer, the vast underground river spans from Wyoming and Nebraska, then south to Texas. It is just outside an area generally considered by geologists to be the border of the Permian Oil Basin. Colton and Paige struggled to operate the 100-acre farm they had inherited from Colton's father, who in turn inherited it from his grandfather they called "Dry Hole" Pete.

Being so far from town meant it was too expensive to have city water piped in. Colton and Paige had to rely solely on the underground water supply from the aquifer and the old well to supply water for their home and few measly livestock, just as great grandaddy Pete did. Like his father, Colton found raising longhorn cattle a pain in his ass. The 100-acre farm was too small to hold enough longhorn to be profitable, plus the longhorn had a nature of seeking out weak spots in fencing to escape. What meat Colton's longhorns did have was much leaner and tougher than typical cattle such as Black Angus, so the herd wasn't a huge moneymaker for him.

Tired of the battles between water, feed, and turning a profit, he began researching alternative livestock to earn more money. Livestock like Emu and Ostrich were both well-suited for the dry Texas heat, plus there was a growing demand for healthier protein sources that required less feed and water. The well's old supply piping and the pump had corroded and were replaced several times over the years, but getting clean water from the well had been increasingly difficult ever since Colton and Paige inherited the land 4 years ago.

The water had always had a foul smell and salty taste, but now the rust, sand, and rattling pipes meant the old well had been showing symptoms of an illness just like a living thing does before it dies. Incredibly, 25 percent of the nation's crops are irrigated with water from the Ogallala Aquifer that ran underneath the farm. However, after decades of snowfall drought in the Rocky Mountains and over-irrigation of farmland further to the north, there was simply not enough water left to reach the farm. The well was dying a slow death, and Colton had no choice but to try to drill for water in another location with no guarantee of finding any.

With borrowed equipment and help from a couple of his high school buddies that worked in nearby oil fields, Colton and his crew began working on the well with the promise of beer and pizza. It was only early summer, but the crew decided to get an early morning start to avoid the intense Texas sun. It didn't really seem to matter what season it was since the sun always seemed more intense as it beat down on the Lone Star state. Colton was hoping to find water about 30 feet down, but just in case he didn't, he planned ahead and brought enough equipment to go twice that depth.

Once the drilling truck was in place, they fired up the auger and went to work. The soil was dry, loose, and sandy, making it easy work for the auger. After only a few minutes, the drill was already 10 feet down. At around 20 feet down,

Colton and his buddies began making comments about the strange smell.

"Damn, Colton, did you bury someone down there?"

"No shit, man, it smells like we dug all the way to hell!"

As they began to back the auger out of the hole, a thick, black goo came right up with it.

"What the hell, Colton, there ain't no water here, but you just struck oil, you lucky som-bitch"! Colton's friend was right.

But how could this be possible? The land had been drilled dozens of times over the last 50 years, and the last geological report from the 1980s said there was nothing under the topsoil but more dirt. They would be lucky enough just to find water. Realizing Colton was about to be richer than he had ever imagined, one of his friends wanted a piece of the action.

"Colton, my brother, we like pizza, but tonight we're havin' the biggest damn tomahawk steaks we can find, fellas!"

As the black crude kept flowing up from the borehole, Colton's emotions swung from excitement to concern. "Oh Hell, Paige is gonna kill me when she gets home. I'm supposed to be drilling for water!"

"Dude, screw the water! You're gonna be able to buy Paige all the water she wants and drink it out by your new swimming pool too!"

CHAPTER 17

The disturbing events that took place at Kim's house earlier that morning, followed by a stop at the campus, had put her and Fred behind schedule, and Wiley was getting concerned. Fred, Kim, and Fritz were still about 100 miles away from Midland when they decided to stop at a truck stop to use the bathroom and eat. When they were done, Fred powered up his laptop and opened his Proton account to send Wiley the blank email he asked for. While Fred was busy logging in to his new email account, Kim was having a tough time letting her guard down and continued to scan the restaurant and parking lot. She didn't like to leave Fritz in the car, but this time, she didn't really have a choice. She ordered a plain double hamburger and some French fries she could take out to him when they were ready to go. His meal of choice when on the road.

Finally connecting to the free WIFI at the truck stop, Fred sent out his encrypted email to Wiley. Following his instructions, all that he had written on the message was a single word in the subject line "OIL." Fred and Kim then tried to relax and ordered some pie and coffee while they waited in a corner booth for a reply. It didn't take long. Within a couple of minutes, Wiley sent his return message. "Go to the nearest gas station or convenience store and buy a burner phone, activate it, and then call me at this number." Wiley typed the number of the new burner phone he had just bought, sent it to Fred, and then turned off his laptop.

As Fred was also closing his laptop, Kim recognized the blank stare of confusion on his face as he took a sip of the bitter, stale coffee. "What's wrong, Fred? What is it? Is the coffee that bad?"

"Oh, no, it's nothing. It's just now I'm supposed to buy a burner phone, whatever the hell that is!"

"Oh Lord, help me, Jesus. A burner is a throwaway phone, Fred. They sell them here at the truck stop."

Fred thought all of this was just a bit too much and that Wiley was perhaps being a little overly paranoid. "We just drove over 700 miles from home. Who the hell would follow someone for 700 miles, and who the hell wouldn't notice being followed for 700 miles!"

Kim rolled her eyes and said, "Well, bless your lil, 'ol heart Fred. How can someone so smart…." She stopped herself midsentence before saying anything that she would later regret.

They had both had a very long, very stressful day, and they didn't see it ending anytime soon. Snapping at each other would only make the day even longer; besides, being snippy wasn't like her, and she felt bad for lashing out at Fred. She normally had a relaxed, easy-peasy personality, but that might be because she had never had to endure this kind of intense stress before, even going through their divorce. Although she still blamed Fred for putting her life in danger, she knew he would never have gone to her house if he had known just how deep the cancer ran.

"OK, honey, so what's the plan? Are we nomads now, just driving across the country with our pet dog like a couple of 1970s hippies?" The mention of hippie made Fred smile as he thought about Jason and the interns, but Kim's sarcasm was thick and felt like a punch right to Fred's stomach, which was already queasy from the truck stop food and stale coffee.

"No, we aren't nomads or hippies, not yet anyway. Rob gave me his new number. I just need to buy the burner and call him. He will give us directions from here."

After a few minutes, he returned to the booth and made the call." Hello, this is Rob." Fred was relieved to hear Wiley's friendly, familiar voice.

"Rob, it's Fred. Can we talk?"

"Yeah, Fred, we should be OK. Where are you?"

"We're at a truck stop just outside of Lubbock heading toward Midland. I hope you have a plan because I sure don't." Wiley went on and gave Fred the address of another truck stop next to an old motel located just on the outskirts of Midland, where they could finally meet in person. Even though he took precautions, Wiley still didn't feel confident that Fred and Kim were safe. He didn't want to risk them leading anyone with bad intentions to his house or his office, so he chose a truck stop outside of Midland for them to meet.

They calculated that driving a mile or two over the speed limit, not fast enough to get pulled over, would make their ETA around 11:30 PM. "OK, that sounds good, Rob. I'm driving a black F-250 Lariat. Keep an eye out for us. We're on the way."

Although he had just under ninety minutes until they would arrive, Wiley didn't want to wait at home and decided to head out to the meeting spot.

Rob was a fan of Adam Sandler, and before he ever left home, he would always remember one of his favorite comedy bits. "Phone, wallet, keys. Phone, wallet, keys. Can't leave home without all of these." This time, however, just as he had pulled the front door open to leave, he realized that there was another thing he needed. If something bad were to happen to him, nobody would even know. He knew he had to tell someone.

Wiley closed the door and went back inside to think for a moment. He really didn't want to bother his dad this late, but the only other person who he trusted, actually the only other person he really knew, was Nate.

Wiley took a deep breath and decided to call his old college buddy to explain to him what was going on. Besides, he thought, if there really was some kind of international oil conspiracy taking place, it could be a huge news story for Nate to break.

"Rob, what's up, my brother! It's a little late. Is everything OK?"

"I don't know, Nate; things are getting a little weird over here with this Ressner guy I've been talking to. I just wanted to let someone know where I was going just in case things continue to go south. Nate, do you remember when I told you about the oil replenishment at my new job site?"

"Yeah, man, that's cool, but what about it? Other than I want to do a special segment on it soon for our local broadcast!"

"Well, I remember hearing about this Dr. Ressner in one of my petroleum engineering classes back in school. He was a legend to some scientists, but most of his colleagues, including one of my professors, thought he was a total nut job. Personally, I'm beginning to believe in the legend over the nut job. I really think the guy is legit. Anyway, I found Ressner's number and called him last night. He was kind of wasted, but this morning he looked at my data and called me back, saying there's a strong possibility we might have a major discovery down here.

Nate, Ressner was getting ready to drive down from Boulder this morning when someone tried to kill him and his ex-wife at her house. He said the guy was a hitman. "Come on, Rob, for real! I mean, that is horrible if that happened, but how do they know it wasn't just some random attempted robbery?"

"Well, because, within the last few weeks, two of his best friends, also petroleum engineers, have been found murdered. And I mean really murdered. No way were these coincidences or accidents. It's pretty gruesome stuff."

"Oh shit, dude, you asked this guy to come to your home? Are you nuts!"

"Yeah, maybe. But I was careful. We have been using burner phones and Proton mail to communicate. I didn't even give him directions to my house or my job site. Nate, he's on the way down from Boulder and should be here within the hour. I'm going over to the truck stop south of town to meet them; I just wanted you to know in case…."

"Hey, don't even think like that, Rob. Listen, I'm going to catch the red-eye flight to Midland and will call you when I land. Rob, thank you for telling me. I may not be a good shot, but I've learned over the years that a well-told news story can be just as effective as a gun."

Once he pulled into the truck stop, Wiley found a discrete parking spot where he could see anyone who pulled in the lot. Slouched down in the seat of his truck, he watched and waited in the darkness. Business was slower than usual at the truck stop. Even for a Tuesday night, there wasn't much activity. These were places that some people have a negative image of, but the hot showers for drivers, hot meals, and enormous lots for them to park their rigs and rest in order to stay below the allowed 11-hour federal driving restriction were havens for truckers. A home away from home for many of them.

After about 45 minutes of watching a few cars come and go and listening to his radio, Wiley was beginning to get sleepy. His eyelids were bobbing up and down, and he felt like they had tiny weights attached to them. Just when he was about to lose the battle of keeping them open for one more second, a large, black SUV with blacked-out windows slowly cruised into the lot. To Wiley, it appeared like a shark circling its prey in the ocean. Rob was concerned because it appeared that the menacing SUV was doing the exact same thing he was doing. Looking for Fred Ressner.

His mind, which just moments ago was exhausted, was now racing out of control. Did Fred screw up the instructions? Did a hitman follow him the entire way from Boulder so he could kill both of them at the same time? But how and why did they find the meeting spot? Wiley hadn't had a good night's sleep in days and knew that he was suffering from sleep deprivation. He remembered from his time in college, with plenty of late nights in the library followed by early morning labs, that one of the main side effects of prolonged lack of sleep is paranoia.

Trying to wake himself from the semi-conscience state, he cracked opened his windows and began taking rapid, shallow breaths, slapping himself repeatedly in the face and talking to himself. He then also remembered that the second sign of sleep deprivation is a form of schizophrenia. Talking to yourself. "Dammit, Wiley, get it together, man. It's probably just some businessperson or a family on a vacation road trip. Chill out." He saw the SUV park across the lot but never saw anyone get out. Maybe they were resting, he thought. Wiley remained in his truck for about 20 more minutes, but he knew that there was no way in hell he could possibly stay awake another 20 minutes, let alone hold his bladder waiting on Ressner.

Looking around the lot and then across at the black SUV, he made the questionable decision to go into the truck stop to buy a high-octane energy drink and empty his aching bladder. After gently sliding out of his truck, he made the painfully long walk with a full bladder from the edge of the parking lot toward the store. He entered the building on the opposite side where the SUV was parked, and as he pulled open the doors, the bright, fluorescent lighting stung his tired, bloodshot eyes. Once inside, he immediately headed to the bathroom, then went straight to the drink cooler to grab a couple of cans of jet fuel he hoped would get him through the rest of the night. After making small talk with the cashier while paying for the drinks, he exited the store the same way he entered.

On the way out of the station, he popped open a can and started chugging it, then waited for the rush. He had only gotten about halfway back to his truck when he heard a man's voice behind him. "Sir, excuse me, sir, but can you give me directions?" Wiley kept his pace but slowly turned his head and saw that the man was still walking toward him. Although he didn't appear to be threatening, Wiley's third eye was already screaming at him, saying this man was dangerous. "Oh, no, I'm sorry, man, but I'm not from around here."

The man had seen the Midland license plate tags on Wiley's truck as he was circling the parking lot, so he already knew that Rob was lying. He knew that he had the right guy. "Oh, really, me neither. Where are you from, buddy? You sound like a local."

Wiley pretended not to hear and didn't answer while he kept his back turned, picking up his pace.

Quickly climbing back up into his truck, he locked the doors and started the engine. He was reaching for the shifter to put the truck in gear when he saw the man pull a gun out from under his jacket and point it straight at Wiley's head. Sleep deprivation was now severely clouding his judgment, but it also probably saved his life. Wiley jammed the transmission into drive and smashed down on the gas pedal like he was stomping out a fire.

The man was close now, only about 15 feet directly in front of the truck. Wiley's truck lunged straight at him, and as gravel flew from the rear tires, the man got off 2 shots that shattered the windshield. With his foot still pressing hard on the gas pedal, the front right bumper of Wiley's truck clipped the man's midsection knocking him to the ground. He rolled several times on the gravel while trying to gather himself, and before he could get back on his feet, the candidate fired off 3 more shots. One pierced a hole in the front driver-side tire, causing Wiley to lose control and veer straight into a shallow drainage ditch that was between the parking lot and the road about 50 feet from the gunman. The back tires were completely off the ground, and Wiley's truck was stuck in the ditch.

Between the rush of adrenaline and caffeine, Wiley was now fully alert. He felt it took an eternity to unbuckle his seatbelt, crawl over to the passenger side door, and slide out of the truck. The candidate was already reloading a fresh magazine holding fifteen .45 caliber hollow point bullets as he continued to casually limp closer toward the truck. Fortunately for Wiley, the angle that the truck went into the ditch had allowed him to slip out the opposite side unseen, and he stammered on hands and knees about 30 feet away from his truck. Once he was able to get on his feet, he ran as fast as he could toward the county highway that ran near the truck stop. He had sprinted about 40 yards down the main highway when the man saw him and began firing at him again. Wiley was by no means an athlete, but he was running faster than he ever had, looking for help from anyone nearby. There was only one vehicle on the road coming in his direction. It was a black Ford F-250 Lariat. Wiley prayed it was Fred as he continued running toward the truck down the middle of the road yelling at the truck to stop. "Fred, it's me! Fred, STOP, it's Rob!"

Ressner slammed on the brakes causing Fritz to fly out of the back seat and crash into the back of Kim's seat. Fred rolled down his window and shouted, "Get in!" Wiley dove into the backseat as the man continued firing at them. Fred knew that if he continued straight ahead, they would be shot. The shooter was clutching his broken ribs, hobbling down the middle of the road, still firing at them. Fred didn't wait on Rob or Fritz to get comfortable. He put the truck in reverse, hit the gas, and backed up as fast as he could go. At about 40 miles an hour, the transmission was whining loudly. When Fred finally felt they were far enough away, he slammed on the brakes while spinning the steering wheel violently to the right leaving an impressive donut on the hot Texas asphalt. He then slammed the truck back into drive and hauled ass away from the killer.

Adrenaline is much more powerful than any energy drink, and now all three of them were jacked up on it. Fred was still flying down the highway until Rob collected himself and calmly asked Fred to slow down. "Slow down! Are you crazy? That maniac is going to kill us! Fred, look in your rearview. He's not chasing us. He doesn't have to. He will find us from the license plate on my truck. I screwed up, Fred. I'm sorry."

"Rob, this wasn't your fault. The only people who knew I was coming to Midland were my 3 interns. Apparently, one of them is a traitor, and I have a good idea which one it is."

Kim said, "Guys, we can figure it all out later. Right now, let's just find somewhere to hide overnight and figure things out in the morning. Hello, by the way, I'm Kim."

"Nice to meet you, Ma'am."

"Well, Rob, any ideas where we can hide out and be safe until morning?"

Wiley knew they couldn't go to his work or his home. He also knew there was a possibility they would connect him to his dad, who lived nearby. But Rob also knew his father. If there was one place they might be able to survive the night, it would be at his ranch. "Well, maybe not entirely safe, but I do know of a place we will at least have a chance. My dad has about as many guns as the 5th group Green Berets."

Behind them in the growing distance, the killer was still watching as Fred's truck veered off the county highway and got onto the Interstate 20 ramp headed east. Even though the truck was soon out of sight, the candidate knew exactly where to find the three.

Rob was giving Fred directions from the back seat while petting Fritz. The combination of Kim's lingering anger toward Fred and the group's exhaustion made for an awkwardly quiet ride, but thankfully the Wiley ranch was only about 10 miles away.

By the time they arrived at his dad's house, it was close to 12:30. The old house was totally dark. Rob felt awful that he was about to disturb his dad so late, especially since they didn't exactly have a close relationship despite Wiley moving back here to spend more time with him. Before they even made it down the long gravel driveway, they saw the lights come on inside the ranch and heard the sound of a barking dog coming from inside the house. A few years earlier, Rob had bought his father a Lacy dog to hunt wild game like raccoons and help pen the small herd of Longhorns his dad still kept around. However, the little dog's companionship had become even more valuable to his dad now.

Wiley was climbing out of the truck when he warned Kim and Fred. "Wait here for just a second. My dad might come out with his 12 gauge." Wiley had walked to within about 20 feet from the house when the porch lights came on, and the front door flew open. Rob's dad had looked out of his bedroom window and didn't recognize the black truck. He could only assume that at this hour, it wasn't a friendly visitor.

"Now, hold on right there, fella. I got a tight choke and four 3-inch shells loaded in this street sweeper. I figure at this range, I can get at least 30 pellets in you before you take your next step."

"Dad, it's me. It's Rob. Don't shoot!"

"Rob? What the hell, son! You almost just got a few more holes put in yer head. Are you OK? What are you doin out here so late?"

"It's a long story, dad? Can we please come in, and I'll explain everything."

"Of course. Come on then; y'all get in the house. I got a bad feeling about this son."

Rob introduced Kim and Fred to his dad, then introduced Fritz to his dog, Lucy. Once the dogs were done sniffing, they immediately hit it off and started playing, chasing each other around the house while the four sat down to talk. It had been a long day, and the story was even longer. Wiley was tired, but he promised to tell his dad what was going on. He thought the least he could do was take the time to explain the situation in as much detail as his father wanted to hear.

"My God, this isn't good, Rob. I don't see any way to cross this river safe if it runs as deep as you say it does. My apologies, ma'am. I don't mean to further upset you or sound like a Debbie Downer here, but y'all know we're all in deep shit, right? Well, you can't go home, you can't go to Rob's, and you can't go to Rob's office. There aren't many hotels in town, and they are probably watching those too. Mr. Ressner, what the hell were you thinking getting my boy involved in this mess, and now you have put all our lives in danger!"

"Dad, it's OK. I asked Fred to come down. It's not his fault.

Rob began to lay out a plan but was interrupted by the two dogs barking.

"Hey, you two, cool it." Speaking quietly now, Rob's dad said, "Hold on, son, I don't think the dogs are playin' anymore. Turn the lights off, Rob. I'll grab all my guns. Everyone, stay in the front room and lie low. And someone, please get those damn dogs to shut up!"

It wasn't uncommon for rural Texans to have several weapons for hunting game and home protection and Rob's father was no exception. He was an avid collector having about every brand, make and model most people have heard of and few that they haven't. He loved the feel and accuracy of his Berretta for hunting turkey and small game, but for home protection, his go-to weapon was his pump-action Remington. Not only did the pump-action sound intimidating as hell, but it had also been configured with a spray pattern that ensured he would hit anything even close to where he was aiming.

Rob's dad thought it would be best to let the dogs stay loose inside the house to eliminate any blind spots like bedroom windows, but the dogs couldn't stop the invasion that was about to take place. Rob didn't know it, but the man who tried to kill him at the truck stop had a partner who had stayed inside the SUV. Together, the two were once again circling their prey, who were now hiding, spread out inside the single-story ranch house.

Outside, it was too dark for the gunmen to use hand signals to communicate. The candidate who was leading the attack was at the front corner of the house began counting down over the headsets the others were also wearing. Taking a position at the back corners of the house, they listened as he began the count down. Three.... Two.... One... On zero, the killer in the back of the house dove through a closed bedroom window, rolled on the floor across the broken glass, and quickly scanned the room for any threats while remaining prone on the floor.

Intentionally hesitating for a split second while the first gunman drew their attention toward the back of the house, the second assassin busted through the front door in an attempt to catch them off guard, but Fritz, Lucy, and Rob's dad were there waiting. Both dogs immediately lunged at the man, and he began to spray bullets wildly around the dark room. Rob's father was less than 10 feet away; he raised his weapon, aimed at the man, and blasted him in the center of his chest with his 12-gauge Remington. Rick was shocked as the blast blew the man's sternum, heart, and spine completely out of his body, leaving a gaping 6-inch diameter hole that went clear out of his back. Rob's father was a seasoned hunter, but he had never seen such massive devastation like this. He was having a hard time choking back the contents of his stomach after seeing what he had done.

Since none of them knew exactly how many men had come for them, Rob's father had to fight his instincts to get down on the floor and army crawl toward the back of the house where his son, Kim, and Fred were still hiding. He knew, though, that if he didn't stay and guard his position at the open front door, they could all easily be killed by a flank attack. By that time, the second killer had got up and slowly began creeping through the open bedroom door into the back hallway, but he didn't even have time to get a shot off. As he took his second step into the rear hall, Fred was there already aiming in his direction. He only had to pull the trigger once to end the nightmare.

The overwhelming combination of noises from the barking dogs, the yelling, and the gunfire had all merged together into a single chaotic scene that overtook Kim. The gangster movies she often watched on television didn't come close to preparing her for the intense, real-life violence, even though it was all over in less than a few seconds. Kim was in a state of shock as she wilted down into a ball, crying on the floor, curled at Fred's feet. Once Kim and the men had time to gather themselves, the four quietly crawled to the front living room to plan their escape. Since they were still unsure of how many men had come for them, they thought making a run for their vehicles parked under a security light in front of the house would be too risky. After a minute of debating the options, they agreed they would call the police, then creep out the back door and try to make it to the nearest neighbor's house on foot.

Based on what Fred and Rob had told him, Rick suspected that their call to the police could possibly be intercepted by someone it wasn't intended for. Whoever sent these killers would be finding out soon enough that they had just lost two more men. Rob's dad calmly dialed 911 and told the dispatcher what had happened. Then they gathered as many weapons and ammunition that they could carry and left the house along with the others despite being told by the dispatcher to stay put. "Darlene, honey, I appreciate your concern, but just send Rambo over, please. We need to get to somewhere safe. OK, everyone, it's about a 2-mile hike through the side pasture. Everyone, keep your mouths on mute, your heads down low, and your eyes open wide for the cow pies. Ma'am, it might be pretty embarrassing to survive a gunfight only to die buried in a pile of cow shit; they are enormous." Rob's dad tried to lighten the situation to help Kim and the group feel more at ease.

Sometimes, even in Texas, the early morning air in May could feel refreshing and cool. Particularly in this part of the state where the air was dry, and there wasn't much around to block the soft breeze that flowed across the flat, desolate land. The air had a pleasant smell of rain coming in, but the lingering, pungent combination of odors from oil and cow manure quickly spoiled it. The slim, fingernail moon wasn't providing much help illuminating the vast darkness to help them avoid the cow pies. It took nearly 30 minutes to navigate their way through the tall clumps of Dallis grass, tumbleweed, cactus, and cow shit to make it to the neighbor's house.

By this time, it was nearly 2 AM, and Rob's dad was beginning to feel awful for what they were about to do. Mainly since he didn't really take the time to get to know his neighbors all that well. All that he did know was what he had heard floating around town. The ranch had been bought by a wildcatter about 100 years ago, and the land had been kept in the family for several generations ever since. There was now a young couple living there who didn't know the first thing about ranching, and the rumor around town was that they were thinking about selling off their small herd of Longhorns and bringing in some kind of oversized exotic birds to breed.

CHAPTER 18

If there was ever an Olympic event for heavy sleeping, Colton would easily take gold. Especially after a few Shiner Bock beers, a favorite across Texas. Unfortunately for Paige, she was not a heavy sleeper, and even after taking an Ambien, an over-the-counter sleeping pill, and a puff on her Delta 8 pen, she often had trouble shutting down her swirling gray matter.

After Colton and his friends discovered oil in his water well earlier that day, they felt a celebration was in order. At around 4:00 PM, they all headed to the nearest grocery store for Tomahawk steaks and more beer. Between the 2 pounds of medium-rare beef and a 12 pack of beer in his belly, by 9 PM, it was lights out for Colton. He had eaten and drank even more than usual, so in addition to the roof rattling snoring, he was now also burping, farting, and drooling so much that the entire side of his pillow was soaked. Paige had lost count of how many times she had begged him to talk to his doctor about his apnea. She told him that he would have more energy during the day if he could get a good night's sleep. However, like most men, Colton would absolutely not go to the doctor unless a limb was falling off, he began growing a second head, or he was pregnant. Paige also had other reasons besides just looking after Colton's health. Her other motivation for wanting him to go see the doctor was her fear of losing her own sanity one night and accidentally waking him up or killing him with a frying pan to the side of the head.

She huffed and puffed and rolled over to give him a stout nudge in the ribs, but once she smelled his bodily functions and saw the drool on the pillow, it was the last straw. "Oh, you're so cute and sexy, baby. I mean, so gross and stinky! That's it. I'm going to the COUCH…. AGAIN" Paige was raising her voice, but Colton could only reply by letting out a grunting, snorting, pig-like noise. She jumped out of bed as fast as she could and grabbed a couple of blankets and pillows from the hall closet; she had gotten them arranged just right on the couch to lie down when she thought she heard something outside. Scared, she tip-toed her way back to their bedroom, where the drunken farter was still sleeping. She got as close to his ear as she could without getting covered in spit or vomit and began with a whisper that quickly escalated, "Colton…. Colton…. COLTON, WAKE UP! Someone is outside!"

"What? Who's there? Paige? What's happening?"

"There is somebody outside, baby!" As Colton was slowly emerging from a beautiful dream that he was with Paige out by their new swimming pool, she had already reached under the bed for their shotgun. While Paige tried to hand it to him, Colton said, "Hang on, hang on. I don't hear nobody Paige; you sure you weren't dreaming."

"How can I dream when I can't even sleep from all of your gross bodily functions? Now, take the dang shotgun!"

Colton's reply was about to roll out of his mouth along with a little more drool and a burp when he heard the knocking on the front door. His stomach sank, and his heart felt like it had been jolted by jumper cables, "Oh shit, Paige, what the hell? There's someone outside!"

She rolled her eyes, saying, "Oh really? You think so?"

"But it's 2 AM! OK, listen. Paige, get your cell phone ready to dial 911. I'm going out there to see what's goin' on. Lock the bedroom door behind me and if you start hearing trouble out there, call Rambo."

Rambo was the nickname of Benjamin Hollister, a high school football teammate and friend of Colton and Paige who had joined the Army right out of high school. To say the least, his parents and friends were shocked when he joined the Army, which explained why he didn't tell anyone until after he had signed all the enlistment papers at the local recruiting office in town. His decision turned out to not only be a good choice for Hollister, but it also made the entire community proud of the sacrifice he had made. He had never really appeared to be any more or less patriotic than any other kid of his age, but that day in September, as he watched the towers in New York crumble to the ground on live television, he made up his mind that he wanted to fight for his country like Chris Kyle from nearby Odessa who became well-known in the American Sniper film.

Hollister's military career began at Fort Benning, Georgia, for boot camp, then onto Fort Campbell, Kentucky, and then on to Fort Bragg, North Carolina, for Special Forces training. He was one of the youngest to ever go through special forces training, so he was affectionally referred to as a Baby Beret by some of the older veterans who were in their 30s. He excelled in the Special Forces and was even nominated for a bronze star for bravery in action. He loved his time serving his country, but after 10 years, he had seen enough carnage in the Helmand and Kandahar provinces of Afghanistan, and he decided not to renew his contract. Even though he was offered a substantial pay increase, a promotion in rank, and more desirable deployments, he had enough.

After receiving his honorable discharge, civilian life wasn't working out quite as he had planned, and he had a hard time finding work as an independent contractor. He was overqualified to be a minimum wage rent a cop, so he endured one gig after another, performing duties as a bodyguard for one rich asshole or another, then eventually joined the Midland Police Force. Hollister enjoyed being a cop, but he didn't like it when people called him Rambo. He thought the people who called him that didn't really understand that the character created by Hollywood was a seriously damaged individual. He wasn't at all like Hollister, who was still grounded by the fact that in battle, he either had to kill or be killed. Not a difficult choice.

Colton made sure there were cartridges loaded in his shotgun while he walked through his dark house to the front door. He flipped on the front porch light, then took a big step back and to the side before yelling, "I gotta gun. Who is it, and what do you want?"

"Colton, it's your neighbor, Rick, Rick Wiley. I know you are probably aiming your Mossberg at the door right now, and I don't blame you, but please hold your fire. I'm really sorry to wake you folks up, but we have an emergency out here. Can we please come in?"

Still shaking off the drowsiness, Colton stood there for a second, trying to figure out if he wasn't still dreaming or really awake; it was all surreal to him. "Wait, who is it again?"

"It's your neighbor Colton, Mr. Wiley. My property line runs along yours. I have the longhorn and a few oil derricks. I helped Paige with a flat tire last year. You remember now?"

"Oh, yeah. Mr. Wiley. Colton tucked his shotgun under his left arm while still holding the stock of the weapon in his hand and began to fumble around in the dark to unlock the old deadbolt on the front wooden door. Finally getting the knob and deadbolt locks open, he was surprised when he saw not only Mr. Wiley but there were also 3 other people, along with two dogs as well.

"Damn, y'all, what's going on? My wife is in the back room about ready to call the cops on you."

The group heard Paige yelling from the back of the house. "COLTON BABY, WHAT'S GOING ON OUT THERE? I'M CALLING RAMBO!"

"Put the phone down, Paige. It's our neighbor, Mr. Wiley. He has some kind of emergency."

Paige was still not convinced. She slowly cracked the bedroom door open just enough so that it wouldn't squeak so she could get a peek into the front room. She wanted to make sure that someone wasn't out there with a gun to Colton's head, making him tell her that everything was OK. She saw Mr. Wiley, but she didn't recognize the other 3 people with him. "Mr. Wiley, are you being held hostage! Do you know those folks?"

"Yes, it's OK, Paige. This is my son Rob and his... our friends. Dr. Ressner and his....this is...it's Kim. We had some trouble at my house and could use some help."

"Colton, are you sure I shouldn't call Rambo now?"

Paige didn't know it, but after the gunfight at Wiley's house, Rick had already called the police. The dispatcher had sent Officer Hollister over to the Wiley house to check things out. Actually, he was probably already there and in a state of shock, looking over the bloody crime scene.

"Hang on, Paige, let's all just take a deep, cleansing breath," this was Colton's thing when he needed to clear his mind, "and talk this out. Y'all come in and have a seat. Paige, baby, can you please grab a jug of that store-bought water and get a pot of coffee going for everyone, please?

"Mr. Wiley, you said you had some trouble at your house. What's goin' on? Was there a fire?"

"Y'all, please call me Rick. No, Colton, it's a little more serious. Besides, I wouldn't give a flyin' flip if that ol' pile of lumber burnt right down to the ground tonight. I'd gladly take the insurance money and have a permanent vacation somewhere down in Mexico. It turns out we were ambushed by a couple of pretty bad amigos, Colton. Dr. Ressner here got himself into a bind, and those sons of bitches tracked him all the way down here from Colorado."

"Holy crap. What kind of trouble are you in, Mr. Ressner? Did you kill someone? Did you steal from the mafia? Bang someone's wife?"

Paige had heard enough and quickly jumped in to shut Colton up by slapping the side of his head. "Colton, baby, have some manners. Can you possibly get any grosser tonight! Please, forgive my husband, y'all. He must still be asleep. Please, go on, Dr. Ressner. What kind of trouble are you in?

"It has something to do about oil, right Fred?" Rob's father said.

Fred introduced himself again to Colton and Paige. Though he felt he owed them an explanation of the situation, he could already see Colton's eyes were beginning to glaze over. Fred knew everyone was exhausted, and he also knew they didn't give a rat's ass if he was a hydro-physicist, a petroleum engineer, or a lumberjack; they just wanted to know what the hell all these people were doing in their home in the middle of the night. Besides, he didn't think there was a chance in hell that Colton or Paige would have any clue what he was about to say. He gathered his thoughts and chose his words carefully so he wouldn't upset them even further.

"First off, please accept my apology for scaring you two in the middle of the night. It seems I've been making some pretty bad decisions lately that have now got all these good people in some trouble. You see, I'm a petroleum engineer, at least I was. I retired, and I am now a professor of renewable energy at the University of Colorado in Boulder. For the last decade or so, before I began teaching, I had been trying to prove a very controversial theory called abiogenic oil creation. Rob and I are probably the only two here that know what that is. Basically, it is a theory that oil is a naturally occurring substance created deep within the earth. It is as abundant as fresh water, and we will never run out of it. Part of my research is to locate oil fields that were once prosperous but had run dry and are now producing oil once again. I know this sounds like science fiction, but".... Fred stopped mid-sentence as he noticed Colton and Paige give each other a blank-faced stare, their mouths and eyes open as wide as the hole Mr. Wiley had just put in the chest of one of the killers still lying in his house. "What? Did I say something wrong? Why do you two look like you've seen a ghost?" Colton and Paige stared back at Fred for a moment before Colton spoke.

"Is this some kind of damn joke! Did one of my friends put you up to this! I swear I will beat someone's ass if y'all think this is funny."

"Whoa, hold on. Are you saying you know what I'm talking about!"

"Hell, yes, I do, Mr. Ressner, and it's been a royal pain in my ass for the last 6 months. You see, my great-grandpa bought this spread back in the late 1920s and got a decent amount of oil out of it, but this land has been dry for at least 30 years. I couldn't even get water out of it that didn't taste like saltwater."

"Saltwater! That's brine, Colton. It's pretty common around large oil reservoirs. You just might be a very rich man soon if my hunch is right! So, that's why you asked Paige to use bottled water. I thought you were just particular about your coffee. But Colton, what do you mean the well WAS dry? Are you saying you're getting oil again!"

Colton slowly got up from his favorite Lazy Boy recliner that had his butt imprinted in the cushion and asked Fred to follow him to the kitchen. It took a few minutes since there was no back pressure in the line, but after he opened up the cold-water knob, they listened to the rattling, gurgling pipes. After a few seconds, Fred's jaw dropped as he saw the thick, syrupy oil begin sputtering and oozing out of the old rusty faucet.

"Does that answer your question, Mr. Ressner?"

"Oh my God. Please, call me Fred. Yes, yes, it does. It absolutely does! I just need to run a few tests on it in the morning to check for impurities to be absolutely positive."

While Colton and Ressner were still talking in the kitchen, the faint sound of a cell phone ringing could be heard in the main living room where the others were sitting. They all began to search for it under cushions, behind the couch, and underneath the coffee table until Rob finally realized the sound was coming from his own back pocket. It was the new burner phone he had bought to communicate with Fred. It was now early in the morning, and Rob's cognitive decline that began many hours earlier was getting even worse. Embarrassed as he pulled the phone out of his pocket, he read the caller ID out loud. "Does anyone know someone named UNKNOWN? The group couldn't help laughing."

"Oh, crap. Unknown. What is it, son? What's wrong?"

"Dad, I only bought this burner so I could call Fred, but if Fred is here, then who the hell could this be?" The others in the group urged him not to answer the call, but it was too late as the green swipe button underneath his thumb was already heading north. "Hello?" "Rob, it's me, brother; it's Nate. We just got to Midland. Where the hell are you hiding, man?"

"Nate, thank God, I totally forgot you were coming. Nate, you said we; who else is with you?"

"Hey brother, I came prepared. I promised my cameraman James a long weekend in Vegas on my dime if he came to record anything we could use for a documentary. Remember what I told you, Rob, I'm no good with a gun, but if James and I can put together a solid story like this one and broadcast it on a major station in a major television market, it can be just as valuable. Besides that, if the story goes viral, it may be even more effective than whacking off a few bad guys. The media is a powerful weapon, Rob. We can bring down the entire empire of evil you told me about."

By this time, Rob was nearly in a coma from exhaustion, but it didn't stop him from laughing out loud at his friend. "Hahaha, dude, it's not whacking off; it's just whacking."

Nate replied, "Tomato, tomatoe. The point is, this sounds like something a local shoot-out will never really resolve; it will only prolong your agony while you wait for your turn for execution. Rob, if I can interview you and Dr. Ressner, I promise this will at least make it on air in Dallas. If it's well-received by the station manager, hopefully, it will be picked up nationally. If that happens, the story will go viral on social media, meaning most of the world will see it within just a few hours, days, or a week at most."

Rob then called out to Colton, who was still talking to Fred in the kitchen, and asked him to come over and talk to Nate.

"Colton, can you please help my friend? My brain is on the verge of a meltdown. He just needs directions here from the airport."

When Colton was done giving Nate directions, he handed the burner back to Rob. Then, they all grabbed a cup of hot, black coffee from the pot in the kitchen and sat scattered around the small, rustic farmhouse. Quietly waiting together in the dim light coming from a single 60-watt bulb in the oven vent hood in the kitchen.

CHAPTER 19

Earlier, at around 1:45 AM, just before the group had finally made their way through the field and made it to Colton and Paige's, Officer Hollister arrived at Wiley's house. He decided to approach the residence in stealth mode. His sirens and warning lights were turned off as he drove slowly down the winding, ¼-mile-long gravel driveway with only his fog lights on.

He first noticed that there were several vehicles parked in front and wondered if Mr. Wiley had company. The house was dark except for one dim light coming from a side room window, not unusual, he thought, considering it was now early on a Tuesday morning. Slowly driving closer to the house, he could now see that the front door was wide open, and there appeared to be something or someone on the threshold, lying partly inside and partly outside on the front porch. Hollister radioed his dispatcher to update his location and possibly a suspicious person. "Dispatch be advised of a possible 10-14 at the Wiley residence."

"Officer, do you need backup?" Thinking at worst he was only dealing with a suspicious person at this point,

Hollister replied, "0-12, standby, please." He would rather send another update once he could get close enough to verify exactly what he was looking at than cause a panic.

Parking as close as possible to the house, Hollister unlocked the Mossberg 500 shotgun mounted to the cage that separated him from the criminals he transported in the back seat. He loaded it with five 12-gauge shells plus one in the chamber, then exited the safety of his patrol car. Cautiously moving closer on foot, he popped the retention lever on his sidearm holster and clicked the safety to red for ready, giving himself immediate access if he needed to use it. With the 12-gauge aimed forward, he learned from military training to not walk directly in front of the intense high beam lights of his patrol car but rather off to the side, preventing anyone inside the house from getting a clear view of him. Now only about 10 feet away with his high beams still illuminating the front door, his suspicion was confirmed as he could now clearly see that it was a body lying in the doorway.

Hollister had been on the police force for several years, and his special forces training, combined with the gruesome scenes he had witnessed during combat, helped him to remain a calm and level-headed officer. However, in the small town of Midland, this type of violent home invasion was rare. He reached for the 2-way radio attached to his shoulder and called in. "Dispatch, I have a 10-87, requesting immediate backup at the Wiley residence." Within only a few minutes that seemed like forever and a day, 3 additional patrol cars carrying officers Reed, Jackson, and Bates arrived at the house.

Without hesitation, they bombarded the front of the house with an impressive, overwhelming amount of white light. In addition to the high beams on all 4 patrol cars, each car was also equipped with a 20,000-lumen spotlight along with another 100,000 candela used for searches and situations such as this. A total of close to 1 million lumens was nearly blinding to anyone trying to look back into it and provided the officers with another level of safety. They could now all clearly see if anyone was still inside the front part of the house before being seen.

The deputies proceeded to surround the house as Officer Jackson took his position at the rear, preventing anyone hiding inside from escaping out a back door or windows. Deputies Reed and Bates stayed with Hollister at the front of the house. As the 3 men crept up the old, creaky steps of the front porch, it became apparent from the gaping wound in the man's chest and the massive amount of blood spatter that he was beyond the need for an ambulance.

The front door was still open from the ambush that went down half an hour earlier, so they yelled loudly inside the little farmhouse to identify themselves. "Midland police. If anyone is here, come out with your hands up." After repeating the warning three times, no reply was given. Hollister knew that between his yelling and light show out front, any element of surprise they could have used to their advantage was now off the table. The three officers would now have to enter the house through the front door to perform a sweep.

Using a special op's technique of room clearing, they each held their left hand on the back of the man in front of him, holding their pistols closely to their chests, pointing down at a 45-degree angle. This technique provided a faster point-and-shoot reaction time compared to having their arms and weapons held straight out in front of them.

The lights, training, and Kevlar vests gave the officers the confidence and the advantage they needed to eliminate any threat before being targeted themselves. Moving quickly and deliberately, officer Bates entered the house and cleared the right side of the room, then the center. Officer Reed was only a half-step behind as he cleared the left side and center, then Hollister, a half-step behind officer Reed, cleared the center and identified himself once more before they all moved deeper inside the house.

Jackson entered through the back door and announced, "Midland Police Department. If anyone is in here, identify yourself now." The officers then spread out as they continued moving from room to room, clearing each one as they navigated through the back of the house that was less illuminated. The enormous amount of clutter made the job difficult as it was apparent Mr. Wiley had become quite a hoarder over the years. Deputy Bates, who was holding his Maglite in his left hand under his right hand that held his 9-millimeter Glock, yelled from the back hallway, "I have a second victim here." Like the dead man lying on the front porch, they didn't see much point in checking for vital signs, considering the two gaping holes in the man's throat and face.

"Clear," said Reed.

"Clear," said Jackson.

"Clear," said Bates.

"Clear," said Hollister.

The officers announced one by one after searching closets and under beds. Once they felt the house was safe, the four officers gathered in the front room, standing in the intense light from their patrol cars. Looking around the crime scene and at each other, they wondered in disbelief what the hell had happened and began to give their own version of the story, no way of knowing just how far from the truth they all were.

·

The search for some type of identification on the dead men came up empty. Hollister then noticed something odd. The fingertips of both of the dead men were smooth, almost like they had been buffed down with sandpaper. He had no way of knowing that the insiders had made the candidates place their fingertips in sulfuric acid. Partly as an initiation but more importantly to eliminate any chance of identifying the men. An oral surgeon under the contract with the insiders had also modified their teeth for the same reasons.

Officer Jackson, who came in from the back of the house, said to all of them, "Damn gentlemen, this is FUBAR. This was not some local meth heads looking to score money or drugs. These guys appear to be professional hitmen to me. They have no fingerprints, no identification, and I guarantee that SUV out front was reported stolen. There's nothing more we can do here. To hell with these dirtbags, let's get the coroner and a detective out here pronto. Our number one priority now is finding Mr. Wiley. Bates, you stay here and help the detective. If he doesn't do it, make sure he scours that vehicle for hair, fingerprints, whatever he can find. Wiley's car is still here, so he must have escaped on foot and gone to the closest neighbor, which is Colton and Paige's house. OK, Jackson and Reed, you two come with me. I'll call dispatch on the way to Colton's and get a missing person's alert out for Mr. Wiley. It appears he defended himself from a home invasion. No offense to Mr. Wiley, but why the hell would anyone invade this dump?"

As the 3 men began to turn and walk out of the house, the faint sound of a cell phone vibrating could be heard coming from one of the dead man's jacket pocket. When Hollister took it out, he noticed something had never seen before; the caller ID was blank. It didn't even display "UNKNOWN CALLER."

"Hello, this is officer Hollister. Who am I speaking to?"

A slow, deliberate, and raspy voice like that of an older man with a pack-a-day cigarette habit replied, "Tell me, Officer Hollister of MIDLAND Texas, are my men dead?" The inflection and manner in the way the man spoke and pronounced Hollister's hometown of Midland not only made him angry, but it also revealed he was speaking to someone very powerful, very far away, and very evil.

"I don't know what men you are referring to."

"You are swimming in deep waters, Officer Hollister. You are already over your head and being circled by sharks.

I suggest you stop being coy with me and answer my question before you are eaten alive. You are using a phone belonging to one of my employees. Now, tell me where he is. Don't make this any harder on yourself than it already will be, Hollister. Are my men dead or not"?

"Yeah, they are dead as hell. Why don't you come and meet me down at the MIDLAND morgue in a few hours and identify the bodies yourself, you son of a...." Hollister heard the click on the line as the old man hung up. One officer asked who it was. "I don't know who that was, but I do know that these dead men worked for him, and he's pissed. Oh, and I think he might have also threatened my life. Guys, I have a bad feeling that there might be more of them coming. I don't know why they are after Wiley, but we need to find him yesterday."

Officer Hollister called the dispatcher again and requested the coroner and detective be sent out and also gave an update on their destination. The three officers then ran back to their patrol cars and headed over to Colton and Paige's, this time with sirens blaring. Rob and his dad were at Colton's house, sitting on the bare wood floor, trying to stay awake. Leaning against the brown paneled wall underneath the front living window alternating between gulping coffee, slapping his face, and glancing out the window, Rob was fading fast. His hand weakened around his cup, and he began spilling coffee on the floor.

Just before closing his eyes, he saw lights moving across the wall behind him, and he raised up to his knees to look out the window. He thought he might be dreaming when he saw the car coming down Colton's dusty driveway. "Hey, is anyone else seeing this?"

Rob's dad said, "Yeah, son, I see it. Y'all get ready; this might be heading south in a hot minute. Grab your weapons and extra ammo. Y'all ready in the back?"

Fred, Colton, Paige, and Kim were spread out all around the house, hiding in the same formation that successfully protected them at Wiley's house as they all called out one by one.

"Ready."

"Ready."

"Let's do this!"

It was then Kim's turn, and she loudly replied, "Bring it on bitches!" Her confidence reassured the group that she was ready. It also signaled to them that she had not only fully recovered from the events of the last 24 hours, but she was also ready to end this.

Rob's father had lost his religion along with his wife many years ago. However, his voice was strong and clear as he told the others, "God bless everyone and good luck. I love you, son." It was the first time in years Rob had heard his dad say those words, and he was nearly overtaken with emotion.

While he wiped away the tear rolling down his face, the group was now alert and wide awake as they kept their focus on the approaching car. As it got closer, Rob noticed an odd, pink glow coming from the front window of the car. His dad saw it too but didn't know what it was. Recognizing the glow of the Uber sign, Rob yelled to the group, "Hang on, hold your fire, everyone. I think that's my friend Nate and his cameraman, James." The car was now slowing down to park in front of the house. As Nate and his camera operator began to get out of the car and grab their gear out of the trunk, the screaming sound of sirens and the flashing red and blue lights of the police cars were coming at them fast. Hollister and his deputies were hauling ass down the gravel driveway, kicking up so much dust they could barely be seen before their antilock brakes finally slowed them from a slide to a full stop directly behind the Uber.

Blinded by the light and overwhelmed by the sirens, the two men instinctively dropped their gear and wisely raised their hands, reaching up toward the dark night sky. "Don't shoot. I'm just a cameraman."

"Well, hell, don't shoot me either. I'm worse. I'm a reporter."

Hollister didn't have any reason to believe either man. It was 5:30 AM, and all he saw were two strangers and a couple of large back duffle bags lying on the ground behind the car. His thoughts went immediately to weapons, and the three officers took dead aim at the two men who suddenly had to pee very badly. Nobody knew what had happened earlier over at Wiley's house except for the police dispatcher. So, Hollister understandably thought that these two could be more killers that intercepted his call and the destination he provided.

"Shut up and get on the ground NOW, spread eagle, hands and feet far apart and face down."

"Officer, please, it's a gravel driveway."

"Yeah, but you will do what you are told if you want to live. Deputy, would you please search these men for identification."

"Officer, I'm trying to tell you I'm a friend of...."

"And I said shut the hell up. Mister, you're not in any position to speak unless I tell you to, understood?"

The deputy took Nate's wallet from his back pocket and read it out loud to Hollister, "Says his name is Nate...."

Before the deputy could finish, Rob's dad yelled out the window, "Officer Hollister, it's. Rick Wiley. It's OK. His name is Nate. He's from Dallas, and he's a friend of my son Rob. He's here to help us."

"Mr. Wiley? What the hell is going on? What happened at your house, and why are you here? We need to talk, sir. If you have weapons, put 'em down and come out front here."

The group was relieved that the police were there. As they all began walking out the front door, the adrenaline was finally beginning to wear off, and exhaustion was creeping back in.

"Hands up and single file, people. Come on out one at a time, please. Colton, Paige? Are you guys OK? What the holy hell is happening here."

"Rambo, you won't believe me when I tell you, but we are OK. You know Mr. Wiley and his son Rob, and this man is Dr. Ressner, and this is his..... this here is Kim."

Hollister pulled Colton aside and whispered, "Colton, I know everyone is tired, and we haven't seen each other in a minute, but please call me Ben or Officer Hollister. This is Deputy Reed and Deputy Jackson."

Colton was now completely sober and could tell that Hollister wasn't playing. He looked his old friend in the eye and said, "10-4 Ben, no problem, I didn't mean any disrespect."

"No worries, Colton, it's all good. If everyone doesn't mind showing me some identification, we can all get back inside and y'all can fill me in on this shit show. I'd also like to know why there are two dead hitmen back at your house, Mr. Wiley."

CHAPTER 20

The atmosphere in the room was uncomfortable and thick as tar even before the old man threw his cell phone into the massive fireplace. Cursing everyone in his sight for their incompetence, the insiders of Argos unanimously agreed that either their vetting process or their assessment of their opponent had seriously failed them. Although the old man had been personally responsible for recruiting many of the candidates, he was quick to deflect blame.

"No shit. You imbeciles have already allowed that fool Ressner, his wife, and now 4 more witnesses to unite, and they all are now under police protection. This is not acceptable, dammit! We now have 3 dead candidates, and Ressner is still running around in cow patty Texas collecting more data and building a God damn cult following everywhere he goes. Telling them he's looking for the blood of the earth or some nonsense. I don't give a damn how many police officers are in that house; I want more men down there NOW and get this situation under control. If another crew is not in that house by dawn, it won't just be Ressner who is dead. We have all the acid we need for all of you."

The insiders of Argos had been watching from overhead, first with satellite, then with remote drones. Tracking Fred and Kim all the way from Boulder to the truck stop, over to Wiley's house, then onto Colton and Paige's. There was nowhere the group could hide that the insiders could not see or hear them. The sophistication of intelligence provided by the team of hackers working for Argos didn't stop when cell phones or televisions were turned off. Microphones and cameras of any electronic device could be remotely activated to gain access to conversations and locations without Ressner, Kim, or any of the group ever knowing. Burner phones and encrypted emails provided no escape even though Rob and Fred thought they were off the grid.

While the five-man crew of candidates scrambled to collect their gear and headed to the airport, the pilot of Citation X was already performing his pre-flight inspection checks. Two of the men who were selected in the group for the mission were former members of 12-man special forces teams. Although special forces typically have redundancy with 2 experts each for communications, medical, demolitions, intelligence, and engineering, these men were chosen because each of them was capable of performing multiple duties. After stowing their gear in the heated, pressurized storage compartment, they boarded the jet.

At a cool $22 million brand new, the Cessna was now a few years old and wasn't as luxurious as other private jets. Several insiders had voted to purchase a Gulfstream G650 for $60 million, pocket change for this group that had accumulated unimaginable wealth. But time was money to these men and the Citation X's top speed of 700 miles per hour allowed them to travel overseas nearly at the speed of sound, wasting as little time on travel as possible. The Citation X was the fastest plane ever built that didn't have missiles attached to it. The insiders often took the jet to meetings, negotiations, and even vacations around the world. Cruising at a speed of 700 would have them at Midland International by 6 AM, cutting it close, but they would have just over 40 minutes to spare before sunrise. The deadline was taken very seriously by everyone on the flight, including the pilot.

The cache of weapons carried onto the jet was mind-boggling, more than enough to take over Costa Rica and would typically have been considered excessive. However, none of the five assassins wanted to experience what they were paid to do to other people. An impressive selection of Sig Sauer, Glock, and Beretta side arms, 3 fully automatic M4 machine guns, and a 50 caliber M107 long-range sniper rifle that launched a projectile with enough mass and velocity could literally cut a man in half from over a mile away.

Colton and Paige lived in a rural area with neighbors that were miles apart, but the crew wanted to complete the mission in darkness to avoid attracting any more attention. The private jet and 2 black SUVs rolling down the south side loop pre-dawn already managed that in the sleepy little town. As the group of contract killers prepared to land, they quickly laid out their plan of attack while studying satellite pictures taken from above Colton and Paige's house and land.

The owner of a local car dealership, who also happened to be a wealthy oil tycoon, had been notified earlier of the arrival of the candidates. He chose wisely not to refuse the request for transportation and agreed to be waiting at the Midland International Airport with 2 SUVs to pick up the team and their gear when they arrived. Transporting them 12 miles to the house, they arrived just 30 minutes before sunrise. Fortunately for the crew, it was a drizzling, overcast morning, and the added darkness would provide the stealth needed as they raided the house.

After being dropped off a quarter-mile from the target, the drivers of the SUVs were ordered to wait while the five men swiftly moved across the waterlogged pasture toward the house. Each man was rucking about 40 pounds of gear on their backs. Wearing all black, they blended into the dark morning sky, making them appear to be nothing more than shadows moving across the field. Immediately taking their predetermined positions, the sniper laid prone behind a tumbleweed about 100 yards from the front door. He quickly unfolded a small aluminum tripod and placed it under his M107 giving him the stability he needed to hold the 35-pound weapon steady. Silently moving close to the house, 2 other men took their positions at the front corners, and the last two men waited for their command at the back of the house. The group inside was unknowingly surrounded by an elite group of killers that left them no way out alive.

While the candidates were moving into position to attack, Hollister and his deputies were wrapping up their questioning inside the house and preparing to head back to the police station. The group was mentally and physically exhausted, especially Rob and Fred, who by now were no longer able to give coherent answers to Hollister's questions anyway. "OK, folks, I realize this has been a difficult ordeal for all of you. We're going to head out now and let you get some rest. We'll be back in a few hours, say around noon, to finish things up. The detective is still over at Wiley's place, but I'm sure he will have a lot of questions for all of you, particularly for you, Dr. Ressner. Until then, I'm going to have Deputy Jackson stay with you all just in case they send someone else for you."

When James, Nate's cameraman, heard that there might be more men coming, he decided he should set up his portable camera and test it for battery life, focus, and lighting while he still had time. He had just placed the camera on his shoulder and hit the record button as Deputy Jackson opened the front door to leave. Jackson had taken just one step forward when he saw the thin red line of the laser coming from the field and froze as he watched it center directly on his chest.

The sniper didn't hesitate; this crew had no fear of the repercussion of killing a cop, knowing that if they failed in their mission, their fate would be much worse than being arrested. The camera was recording as the massive half-inch diameter by 2-inch-long round exploded out of the 50 caliber M107 and struck Jackson in the abdomen, easily penetrating his Kevlar vest like it was no more than a sheet of paper. Known as an anti-material projectile, the energy of the bullet launched Jackson backward, slamming him against the living room wall as it instantly liquified his internal organs. Once it had passed through his body, leaving a softball-sized exit wound, it continued on its path, leaving another hole as it passed through the living room wall, then another hole as it finally exited the back of the house.

Hollister yelled, "Everyone to hit the floor and get behind something." He knew this had little chance of improving their chance of survival. However, his intense and extensive combat training instinctively had him take command, not freeze like most people would do when faced with such gruesome brutality. Colton quickly hit the light switch leaving the front room dark, but there were still a few more lights scattered around that gave the sniper a clear view into the house.

Without hesitating, Deputy Reed, Wiley, and Kim grabbed shotguns and began shooting the lights out around the house. In nearly total darkness now, the group crawled on the floor and collected the cache of weapons and ammunition that was still scattered around the house while James hit the night vision mode on his camera and continued to record.

Looking out the front door that was left open by Officer Jackson, Fritz saw movement from the sniper lying in front of the house. He bolted out of the house while Kim fought the urge to scream out his name to make him return to her inside. Lucy followed him in stride. As the two hunters raced at full speed ahead toward the sniper, they saw another flash of light from his rifle but continued toward it as fast as their four legs could carry them.

The sniper was the only member of the team with the foresight to pack his night-vision goggles, and he was now targeting the dogs before they could get to him. Fritz and Lucy were moving fast, weaving between tumbleweed and cactus in the cover of the pre-dawn darkness. The sniper tried, but he couldn't hold the two in his sight long enough to get off another shot. Lunging at him in attack mode, the extensive damage done by the pair of trained predators was brutal. The candidate screamed for help in horror as they began eating him alive, ripping and tearing the flesh from his face, neck, and hands.

The two assassins near the front corners of the house couldn't see the attack, but they could hear the terrifying screams and knew the exact location of the sniper. They began shooting blindly in his direction, hoping to scare the dogs off. While they missed hitting anything, they were giving away their location to the group inside the house.

While the insiders were firing at the dogs, Colton saw the flash of light from one of the killers' guns coming from just underneath the bedroom window he was crouched next to. Colton gently laid his shotgun on the wood floor and then reached for some old rope he had mounted on the wall next to a picture of his great-grandpa Pete. He wrapped one end of the rough, weathered rope around his right arm several times, then braced himself by placing his size 14 left Tecovas boot against the windowsill. Slowly, he lowered the lasso around the killer's neck, and before the assassin could react, Colton quickly jerked the loop tight and hoisted the man completely off the ground. His feet were swinging wildly, banging and kicking against the house as he gargled and choked. He tried to yell for help, but his own body weight had made the noose too tight for any air to go in or out. At 6 feet 5 inches and 260 pounds, inactivity had resulted in Colton putting on a little weight since his high school football days, and he was using every ounce of it. Colton pushed off the windowsill and jerked the rope again, causing the assassin to drop his weapon as he tried to squirm out of the dry, scratchy old rope cutting deep into his throat. While the man was hovering about 2 feet off the ground, Colton used his leverage once again and gave the rope a final, hard jerk. He heard the man's neck snap, killing him instantly. A distant, long-forgotten memory of his own leg breaking as he was tackled flashed through his mind when he heard the man's neck bones cracking.

Hollister then reached for his shoulder-mounted radio and quietly called in a Code 3 that would have dispatch sending all available units with sirens on and lights flashing to respond to the emergency. Since it was now past 6 AM, fresh officers had just logged in when the call went out. Within minutes, a half dozen officers were flying toward Colton and Paige's house.

The last three remaining candidates were running out of time and knew they had to complete the mission and get out of sight while they still could. They were now using microphones and earbuds to coordinate a simultaneous attack from 3 corners of the house. James continued recording the events as they unfolded, but the chaos was so scattered he was having a tough time following the action. The recording was made even more difficult as he remained safely hidden behind Paige's heavy wooden dining room table that he had flipped over to provide protection from the gunfire.

Just as he decided to crawl out from behind the table for a better angle, the shooter in the front corner of the house dove through the dining room window directly behind him, rolled onto his knees, and quickly pointed his gun at Fred, shooting him in the back and dropping him to the floor. With 13 bullets left in his magazine, the gunman then turned to fire at James. Before he could get off a shot, Kim blasted him at direct range in the chest. His Kevlar vest stopped the pellets, and the impact only knocked him backward a few feet. As he stumbled to gather himself, he turned his weapon toward Kim; but just before he could get another shot off, Mr. Wiley and Officer Hollister opened fire, shooting him in the face and neck numerous times. The blood was spurting across the room like a red super soaker as he staggered on his feet around the dark room, bouncing off of walls and furniture. The bizarre scene resembled a zombie scene in a horror movie until he finally collapsed dead onto the floor.

Fritz and Lucy were still working on the sniper a hundred yards out in the front yard, so the two remaining killers in the back of the house were out of their line of sight. As dawn was approaching, the two men in the back could now see each other positioned at opposite sides of the house. Using hand signals again so the group wouldn't hear them, they met in the middle of the house and began to slowly walk up the creaky old stairs. Climbing onto Colton's warped back porch, they quietly pulled open the aluminum door, then slipped inside the house.

Kim had crawled about 15 feet on her hands and knees across the wood floor that was made slick from what seemed like gallons of blood. As she checked on Fred, James felt less than human as he reluctantly recorded the moment. The emotional, deeply personal scene of Kim crying over her dying best friend, lover, and father of her children was hard to watch, but James felt that it might be needed as evidence. "Dammit, Fred, don't you do this. You can't leave me now." It took every last ounce of strength she had in her petite, exhausted body to roll Fred over onto his back. When she did, she saw that the exit wound from the bullet was close to his heart, a fatal wound, but somehow Fred was still breathing. Kim took him by the hand as he gently squeezed it while saying his 4 last words to her. He first said I love you. He then said Henry. Kim thought nothing about the name Henry thinking Fred may have been hallucinating. As she looked into the blank stare of his coal-black eyes, he released his final breath.

The chaotic scene around her was fading into a silent, slow-motion nightmare as she blocked out everything around her to focus on Fred. She laid her tired head on his bloody chest while the memories of their life together flashed in her mind. The last two candidates continued moving slowly and silently through the house. Once they were in position in the back hallway, they began their final silent countdown to zero, then used the same left, right, and center room-clearing technique that Hollister learned in the military and later taught his deputies, they attacked.

The room was beginning to lighten, but the group was still well hidden. Neglecting to pack night vision for the mission, the killers' eyes were strained and squinting from the dim light and the sulfur. They surveyed the carnage and could only make out the 3 dead bodies and Kim lying on top of Fred.

Rod enhanced vision allowed Fritz and Lucy's eyes to clearly see in the darkness and straight into the open front door of the house. When they saw the two killers moving from the back hall into the front room of the house, they abandoned the sniper and began racing back toward the open door. Running into the house, they paused and were growling loudly at the killers alerting the others that there were more men inside. Sadly, their warning also gave the killers the location of the dogs. As Fritz and Lucy lunged toward the two men, they fired several shots in their direction, one hitting Lucy in the chest.

Shooting at the dogs again proved to be another fatal error by the killers as the flash of light from their weapons gave the others a fraction of a second and just enough light to see where the men were, and the group opened fire at them. Aiming toward the flashes of light, an overwhelming gauntlet of gunfire rained down on the two men from Hollister, Rob, Rob's father, Colton, and Paige while James kept recording. Blindly returning gunfire around the dark room, two random bullets hit Hollister, one in his Kevlar vest and another in the upper thigh, while another penetrated Paige's left arm at her biceps muscle. The body armor worn by the killers had provided little protection as so many rounds from shotguns and rifles were fired by the group in the direction of two men that when they finally dropped to the floor, their faces appeared to be nothing more than bloody, dark red sponges.

Their ammunition had nearly run out, and the intense smell of sulfur gave the small room the smell of a fireworks factory, and the floor was littered with dozens of plastic and brass casings. Not hearing or seeing any more gunfire, the group ceased fire. The ragtag group who had all met only a couple of hours earlier had somehow just eliminated two more professional killers, the last two they thought would be coming for them. Remaining alert, still not knowing for sure if they were safe, the group was given a sign of hope as they heard the distant sound of the backup police cars that were now flying down the muddy driveway. The light rain had finally ended, and the sun began to peek over the flat Texas horizon. The haze inside the house was so thick that it burned their eyes, causing them all to squint. Even with the rising sun, they could now only see slightly better than if they were still in total darkness. Their ears were ringing loudly from the shoot-out in the small house, and looking around the dim room gave them all a feeling of despair.

The tragic loss of Fred was devastating to everyone. The contradiction between his death and the arrival of the officers, along with the new morning sun, gave the group a strange, surreal combination of emotions. Accomplishment and hope yet also a deep, dark sadness. The entire siege was over in less than 10 minutes, but the emotional and physical damage was severe. Hollister was in agonizing pain and gravely wounded, but during the chaos, he had heard the distant sound of sirens of the backup officers getting closer. As he lay bleeding profusely on the dirty hardwood floor, he was somehow able to once again reach for his radio to call the officers and let them know it was safe to enter before he blacked out.

"This is Officer Hollister. 10-26. All clear. Dispatch, we need EMS and ambulance support ASAP."

Hollister removed his belt and wrapped it around his leg to slow the bleeding down. As he looked around at the devastation, it brought a brief flashback to another gun battle he was involved in Afghanistan several years earlier. He hoped then that he would never have to see this type of violence ever again. The dust was still settling inside Colton and Paige's haze-filled, bullet-ridden, blood-soaked house when the additional backup officers stormed onto the scene. Although they had heard Hollister's all-clear call go out over dispatch, they still had a job to do. So, the 6 heavily armed Midland officers pulled up to the house like their hair was on fire.

With very few exceptions, most local police and EMS are typically incredibly responsive when a call goes out for medical support but maybe even a little more so when one of their own is in trouble. Having no way of knowing for certain if there was still a threat inside the house, the backup officers did exactly as Hollister and his deputies did at Wiley's house and gave an order. "This is the Midland Police Department. Put your weapons down and come out single file with your hands up." Hollister heard the command, and before he blacked out, he instructed Colton to help and take Paige first out the front door where the officers and EMS were waiting. Once they were clear, he then asked Rob, then his father, and finally Nate and James to all put their hands up high and slowly walk one at a time out the door.

The officers ordered the four men, along with Colton, to lie face down on the wet grass, but nobody complained as the damp, wet grass felt cool and refreshing on their skin. One of the EMS teams immediately laid Paige down in the back of an ambulance and began working to stop the bleeding from her right arm. The bullet didn't hit any bones, major veins, or arteries but had torn clean through her biceps, causing the distal tendon to be ripped from her forearm, leaving it dangling by her side. Hollister was now fading in and out of consciousness as he continued losing a massive amount of blood. He was somehow able to look over and see that Kim was in shock, still lying over Fred's dead body. Knowing that she would have to be pulled off of him, he made his final call for assistance before he lost consciousness. This time the call of his name and badge number was received by dispatch, and all the officers, including his former partner on the force who knew Hollister well, instantly replied that they were coming in.

Two deputies remained outside with the group while the others entered the house to witness a crime scene like nothing any of them had ever seen before, including seeing one of their own, Officer Jackson, lying in a puddle of blood with a gaping hole in his back. Two officers cleared the house and confirmed that all of the assassins were dead, while the other two helped the EMS put Hollister on a stretcher and then took Kim outside for treatment. Once the five men, Rob, his dad Rick, Nate, Colton, and James, had been cleared, they were all released from their handcuffs. However, all remained sitting in the damp grass in front of the house, unable to move as each of them replayed the horrific events of the night over and over again in their heads.

CHAPTER 21

The old man pushed the "UP" button on the 8-foot retractable screen, turned off the high-definition projector, then sat in silence after watching his entire plan disintegrate before his eyes. Many members of Argos had tried, but only a few had learned the true identity of the old man, and they would never divulge the information for fear of the frightening repercussions. His decades-long reputation as the most ruthless member of the group had been enough to protect him. Most of his colleagues believed he was a descendant of one of the original oil barons, but his skin tone and accent made it difficult to identify his heritage. He had homes in several countries around the world and would use his vast wealth to move between them as he wished. As one of the founders of the Insiders group within Argos, he was still an extremely dangerous and powerful man, but the young blood didn't care about who he once was. All they knew was that he was slipping, and something had to be done to stop him.

After the meeting of the 100 Argos members adjourned the previous day, a small group of six Insiders stayed in the mansion overnight. They gathered early the next morning to watch a live video stream of the raid in the grand study. They watched the event closely while it was being transmitted to them by a drone they had contracted to provide the live feed. Each member of the five-man team of candidates that were sent to kill Ressner had been equipped with communication devices that enabled the group to listen in. As each killer was eliminated one by one and the audio of each was replaced with either static or silence, the likelihood of the old man surviving the day was also fading fast.

Beginning at Kim's home in Boulder, then down to Rick Wiley's ranch in Texas, and finally to Colton and Paige's, the Insiders were stunned as they had watched and listened while 8 elite, highly-trained candidates were eliminated. With each death, the anger grew in intensity within the group. The old man had personally selected many of the candidates and knew that he would now be a target himself unless he could somehow present a contingency plan that could save himself from a certain brutal death. After reminding the others of his successes with eliminating both Crick and Smythe, he began to offer the group a scheme he hoped would save what little time he had left.

"Gentlemen, I agree that the events of this morning are disappointing to all of us; however, Ressner is dead. The goal of this morning's operation was to eliminate Ressner, not kill any more innocent people than we already have. We have monitored his classroom lectures and canvased his students. Yes, most of them liked Ressner, but they also thought he was a nut. And thanks to our colleague at the university who arranged to plant a young man named Henry in his inner circle, we are also aware of Ressner's communications with his interns. While they also seem to like the man, none of them have any desire to follow in his work.

There is nothing more we need to be concerned about. We have cut off all three heads of this pest. Crick, Smythe, and Ressner. However, we also know there is one remaining witness that must be dealt with. We have his name, and we have his address. Gentlemen, we know where and how to find Mr. Wiley. He can run, but he cannot hide from us, not for long anyway. We need to assemble another crew immediately and eliminate this virus before it has time to spread again."

The Insiders of Argos were a callous gang, void of the human emotions of sympathy or mercy. While they squirmed in their seats, reading the expressions on each other's faces, the old man began to sense that his fate would indeed have the same ending as the others he had made examples of. Either by shooting, dissolving in acid, decapitating, or cutting into pieces, he would not live to see the end of the day. It was becoming obvious from their reaction to his plea that the other five members were not impressed by his plan, but they had no other options. Either they could wait and see if

Wiley would continue on with Ressner's work, or they could kill him before he had a chance.

The dossier compiled by the Insiders told a story of a man with nothing to lose. Rob Wiley was a single man with no kids, no pets, no friends, no mother, and a fractured relationship with his father. He had recently relocated from Houston to Midland and worked for a small drilling company. He was a loner, the type of man that nobody would notice if he were gone, let alone miss him. The discussion of whether or not to kill another man was held casually while they ordered breakfast. Planning Wiley's murder had as much effect on them as if the hollandaise sauce on their eggs benedict had enough lemon juice.

Once they had finished their breakfast, a decade younger and much more energetic insider named Fadi spoke. He had a fast, high-pitched, middle-eastern accent; before taking a sip of his coffee, he said, "Very well, we will eliminate the virus as you call it, but this time you will not be involved in choosing the candidates for this mission. You have been living off your past successes long enough. Including what you did with Stanley Meyer back in '98. You are now officially retired."

With that statement and a nod to a candidate Fadi always kept by his side for protection, the old man was escorted away, never to be seen or heard from again. "Gentlemen, let us enjoy our meal before it gets cold. If no one objects, I will coordinate my own team to resolve the matter of Mr. Wiley since our esteemed colleague could not." With no objection from the other men, the five went their separate ways only to meet again the following month at another secret location.

Forty-five minutes later, back in Midland, Hollister was undergoing emergency lifesaving surgery. The triage he received from the EMS while being rushed to the hospital saved his life. Now, the surgeons at Midland Memorial were trying to save his badly mangled leg. The first 45 caliber round that struck him had nearly penetrated his Kevlar vest and left a massive, swollen contusion on his sternum.

The second round penetrated his right thigh just below the hip joint blowing out a two-inch chunk of his femur. The force of the impact of the 45 caliber was so violent that it caused his leg to swing out from under him and arch wildly backward so far that he nearly kicked himself in the back. The bullet had missed both his scrotum and his femoral artery by only a fraction of an inch. Less than a centimeter was all that separated Hollister from being castrated or killed. He had been severely wounded, but after the successful surgery to remove the bone fragments, inserting a titanium rod held in place by 4 screws, then with weeks, possibly months of physical therapy, he would fully recover ahead of schedule and return to the police force.

That afternoon in the same operating room, Paige also underwent a complicated surgery. After the surgeons repaired the hole in her biceps and reattached it to her forearm, she also had months of physical therapy ahead of her.

The realization of just how close he was to losing his high-school sweetheart resulted in an immediate transformation in Colton, and he vowed to change his lifestyle habits; he even went to the doctor to have his snoring condition treated. Back at their ranch, Colton picked up back where he and his friends had stopped, and within 3 months, he was producing more oil than Dry Hole Pete ever did. Paige didn't want to return to the house, let alone live in it after what had happened there, and Colton agreed. Using the profits from his new thriving oil business, he gladly bulldozed the house to the ground. In its place, he built another with enough room for 11 kids. Big enough for his own football team. Paige wasn't disappointed that between the massive house and the new inground swimming pool that Colton also had installed, so much space was taken that the Emu and Ostrich ranch had to be put on permanent hold.

Kim stayed in Midland another day to coordinate the return of Fred's body back to Colorado. After the arrangements were made, she wanted to fly herself and Fritz back to her Colorado home, but she didn't know what to do with

Fred's truck. It was a large, lifted truck with oversized wheels, and Kim didn't think she could safely make the 10-hour drive back home alone in her state of mind driving the enormous truck. She was thinking over her options during breakfast at the local Waffle House, a drastic change of pace for the healthy hiker, but she desperately needed comfort food. She had got about halfway through her pecan waffle and was about to take a sip of coffee when the bell on the front door jingled, and two familiar faces walked in.

Rob and Rick Wiley and Kim made eye contact simultaneously, and Kim quickly slid out of her booth and ran toward the two men. Tears that had welled in her eyes began flowing down her face as the two heroes became blurry before she could get to them and give them both hugs. Other customers noticed and stared as the three could hardly hold back the tears while walking back to Kim's booth to talk. She hadn't had a good night's sleep in days; after the raid, she felt like her emotions were on the edge of a very high, very steep cliff, and she was barely hanging on. Though not physically injured during the raid, her recovery from the emotional trauma and the depression that would follow meant her healing process would take a lifetime.

Rob and his father had spent the night together at Rob's house and the next morning had gone back to Rick's to assess the damage to the old ranch and talk about what they should do with the house and land. The death of Gina years earlier and what had occurred the previous day made Mr. Wiley unsure if he wanted to return to the place that had so many bad memories attached to it. "Rob, I have an idea. Why don't you and I drive Miss Kim back to Colorado? We need to get out of here for a while anyway, and this would help all of us out. What do you say, Kim?"

"Oh, no. I couldn't possibly ask you to do that, Rick. It's a ten-hour drive, and I have Fritz!"

Rob then provided the perfect reply that his father was hoping for. "With respect, ma'am, but you don't need to ask us; we would love to do it. My dad is right, we both need to get out of town for a bit to clear our heads, and this will give dad time to decide what he wants to do with the ranch. We can head out whenever you're ready!"

While Rob and his dad were wolfing down 2 Allstar breakfasts, Kim took her leftover waffle and two orders of bacon out to the truck where she had left Fritz waiting in the cool comfort of the air-conditioned truck. After a quick stop at Rob's and then over to Rick's, they each packed a bag before hitting the open road heading up Highway 349 toward Lubbock. There was finally a sense of calm and safety inside the truck as if they were leaving all their problems in the rearview mirror. Nobody noticed as the Citation X came in for a landing at the Midland International Airport just outside their tinted windows.

Rob set the cruise control to 80, and with very little weekday traffic, they were near the outskirts of Amarillo in 3 hours when Rob got a call from Nate. After being questioned and cleared by the police, Nate and James were allowed to fly back to Dallas. They had been working non-stop editing the video James recorded during the raid, and now Nate needed a story to go with the raw footage. "Honestly, Rob, I'm not sure how much of this we will be able to air on live television. It's pretty intense. The footage is important to emphasize that this isn't a conspiracy and that it is real. We can blur out a lot of the more sensitive parts, but I need the back story, my brother. Rob, what in God's name have you gotten yourself into?"

The three were close to the junction of Interstates 40 and 24 when Rob pulled the truck over and asked his dad to take over driving. He needed to focus on the details Nate needed for his story. For the next 90 minutes, he gave his friend detailed information on oil field replenishment and the theory of biogenic oil creation. He even forwarded Nate the email he had sent to Dr. Fred that contained the proof that Crick, Smythe, and Fred had all died for. Nate was well paid for his gift of gab and his ability to remain calm under pressure while sitting in front of a live television camera. Not being able to find the words that typically rolled from the tip of his tongue was unusual for the television news anchor, yet by the end of the call, he was speechless.

Nate knew that Rob was in trouble, but he didn't know they were still being monitored. Calling Rob on his personal cell phone had just poured gas on the wildfire, and it was now about to spread further east toward Dallas as their conversation was intercepted by two hackers working for Argos. Before ending the call, Nate shared some good news with his friend, "Rob, James, and I met with the general manager of the station late last night while we were editing the footage. He's 100% all in. This is unheard of, but he has already spoken to the owners, and they have arranged for a simulcast of our segment to go out live to all the stations they own. After watching the graphic footage and hearing my lame attempt trying to explain the backstory to him, he said this could possibly earn the station another Emmy for the best regional documentary of the year. Rob, the owners of this station have 10 more major market stations across the country. This story is about to blow up. Hopefully, it will be picked up by a national news network for a re-broadcast, but at the minimum, it will be aired over every social media platform around. James and I were given an entire team to confirm your data, research, write, edit, and condense this entire story into a 7-minute segment that he wants ready for broadcast on live television tonight before any one of our competitors gets wind of it. This is huge, Rob. I'm sorry that it won't bring Fred back, but at the minimum, this story will give Dr. Ressner, Crick, and Smythe their reputations back, and from what you have told me, it could be the beginning of the end of generations of lies. Rob, I have to get cracking on this; having it ready for airing by 6 will be a major undertaking. This is considered a documentary that we typically spend weeks or months putting together, but between our footage and your information, we should be able to create not just a quality segment but, more importantly, a believable one."

"Nate, please email the finished product to me before it airs. I might not get to see it before we get back to Boulder."

Within seconds of ending their call, one of the two Argos hackers who were listening to the conversation was in contact with Fadi with an update, and it was not the news he wanted to hear. The message meant that Fadi would have to make a difficult decision as their intended target was now halfway to Colorado, and another witness to the raid, a well-respected news anchor, was preparing to broadcast a damaging story on Argos. The video of the raid would be shown on live television in eleven major television markets in just under 6 hours.

In a dramatic turn of events, Fadi had also underestimated the complexity of the situation, just like the old man he had murdered just hours earlier. He often turned to his religion for guidance; he held his hands high, looked to the ceiling, and said a prayer for strength and forgiveness for the past sins he had committed. "Astaghfir Allah likuli dhanubi wa'atawajah 'iilayhi." As quickly as he called on his faith for guidance, he lost his religion even faster. "Why don't these bastards just die!" He then picked up his cell phone and called the leader of his hit squad.

"This is Fadi. Have the pilot get the Citation ready and get your crew over to Dallas now. This reporter must not succeed." Fadi was already feeling the heat, and it was quickly getting hotter than the scorching desert sand of his home country.

"Sir, that won't be possible, at least not in the Citation. We blew out a tire on landing, so we need to wait at this airport overnight for a replacement."

"We don't have overnight, dammit. Rent a car and drive to Dallas if you have to. You have under 6 hours to stop that broadcast. And sergeant, do I need to remind you what will happen to you and your crew if you don't make it in time?"

CHAPTER 22

Rob, Rick, and Kim had made good time from Midland, but they were still about 90 minutes away from Boulder
when Rob's cell phone chimed, alerting him of an incoming
email. The subject line read "Blood of the Earth," and there
was a large file attached. Rob knew it had to be the 7-min-
ute segment that Nate had promised to send to him before it
went live in Dallas and the 10 other stations that agreed to air
it. One station happened to be in Denver.

Although he now had the segment downloaded on his
phone, Rob wanted to find someplace they could all stop
to watch it on live television so they could celebrate. Rick
had been driving Fred's truck since they had pulled over in
Odessa and was now looking for a restaurant or hotel where
they might be able to watch the broadcast at the bar or in the
lobby. While searching for a place to stop, Rob just couldn't
wait any longer to watch the video, but just as he began to
open it, he received an incoming request from an unknown
caller wanting a video chat.

The Wiley men had a distant relationship, but Rick knew his son, and he recognized that the blank stare and suddenly blood-red cheeks told him something was wrong. Rob braced himself, then reluctantly accepted the invitation. He immediately regretted his decision and became overwhelmed with anxiety when the caller's image was displayed on the 6-inch touchscreen of his cell phone. The caller was using a modulator to disguise their voice and a full-face Punisher face mask to hide their identity. The Punisher character from movies and television series had been one of Rob's favorite vigilantes since he was just a kid but seeing someone wearing the disguise and using an altered voice had a terrifying effect on all three of them.

There are occasions in all our lives when we understand why we were given just one mouth but two ears. This was one of those times, and Rob wisely chose to listen more than he spoke. The anonymous caller was a step ahead of him and controlled the conversation from beginning to end as Rick and Kim closely listened from the front seat of the truck.

"Mr. Wiley, don't let the mask and voice disguise alarm you. In the last 48 hours, you all have gotten a taste of what these maniacal extremists are capable of. Politics, borders, and laws are of no concern to them. Their only motivation is money, and they control 99 percent of the world's wealth.

Doctors Crick, Smythe, and Ressner had challenged and threatened their main income stream, oil, for decades. These three men backed the beast into a corner until it had no choice but to strike back. I am here to tell you that the beast will soon have a new nightmare to deal with. Rob, Rick, and Kim, you have friends who you don't know. Our plan will succeed, and soon you and your families will no longer have to look over your shoulders in fear. I will be in touch later tonight. Please, keep your cell phone on and with you."

"But who are...." Before Rob could even finish asking who he was talking to, the call abruptly ended.

The three looked at one another, hoping that someone would have a clue who the person could have been, but they were all dumbfounded. Tossing out wild theories, they all began laughing when their guesses eventually became increasingly absurd as they went from Jimmy Hoffa to the Pope. It was the first good laugh any of them had in days, and it was therapeutic to them as they continued guessing.

"It was an alien," Rick said.

"Na, it was Waldo!" said Kim.

"Hey everyone, there's a Hilton up ahead. Maybe we can watch the broadcast there," Rob said.

They had only a few minutes before the evening news would begin, so Rick parked under the canopy near the front lobby. The three ran inside together, scaring the front clerk. She was working alone at the front desk and was watching Peaky Blinders on a small television. Kim calmly explained, "We are so sorry to alarm you, ma'am, but we have an emergency. Can you please turn the television to Channel 31?"

She refused to change the channel because they weren't guests at the hotel. Besides, she was watching Peaky Blinders. Just before Thomas Shelby gulped down another shot of Irish whiskey, she quickly changed the channel when Rob pulled out a $20 bill and handed it to her. They all stood close together and waited for the broadcast to begin.

Like most major market television stations preparing for a live broadcast, the KDAA studio in Dallas was beginning to resemble a human beehive with just a few minutes remaining until the red glow of the camera and hot, bright studio lights came on. The general manager of the station, along with the entire news crew, including Nate and his co-anchor, the sports and weather anchors, desk editors, cameramen, producers, segment directors, and writers, had just gone into their pre-broadcast briefing. This is usually a casual briefing to discuss the standard operating procedures and review or make any last-minute changes to the segment board before the broadcast goes live. This meeting was much more rigid, however, and the General Manager emphasized he had no wiggle room on time slots. The GM instructed the weather and sports segments to cut their time short to allow room for the 7-minute segment James and Nate had only completed just an hour earlier.

While the news team was making their final preparations, another team that had begun speeding toward Dallas like a bat of out hell six hours earlier was now just a mile away from the station, barreling down Interstate 30. Coming in hot to the television station parking lot with their tires squealing, the men bolted out of the rental car, popped the trunk, and began arming themselves. They had less than 5 minutes before it would be too late. To their advantage, many local news stations do not have metal detectors or security guards to keep out unwanted visitors. However, after the general manager watched the video James shot of the raid and Nate's warning of the potential for sabotage, he called a temporary staffing agency earlier that day and had a guard sent over. He was seated at the front entrance and instructed to keep the glass double doors locked.

Nate and the other anchors were now taking their places at the news desk while the floor manager did a quick final check of their microphones, cameras, and teleprompters. The most important broadcast of Nate's career was about to begin as the director began the backward countdown out loud at first, then silently as she got to 3, 2, 1. As soon as the camera's red light came on, she pointed at Nate to begin. "Good evening, and welcome to tonight's broadcast. I'm Nate…." Before he could get out his last name Jones, the sound of breaking glass could be heard coming from the lobby when the killers shattered the front doors.

Glass doors and a semi-retired, morbidly obese security guard were no match for the candidates. They kicked in the door and shot the guard in the face before he could even unholster his weapon hidden beneath his distended belly that overlapped his gun belt. The popping sound of the gunfire echoed throughout the newsroom, and Nate's stomach sank while he sat frozen in front of the live camera. The men had caught the entire staff off guard as they made their way from the lobby to the studio floor in only a few seconds. Faster than the producer could stop the live feed and go to a commercial. Several of the floor and control room crew began screaming and hiding for cover under desks and behind equipment as the masked killers ran with their guns drawn and took aim directly at Nate, who was still on live TV. The general manager was running across the control room and was reaching to hit the kill button when one of the Candidates shot at him but missed. "LEAVE THESE FUCKING CAMERAS ON OR EVERYONE IN THIS ROOM DIES."

Fadi had intentionally neglected to inform the other insiders of his plan to assassinate Nate on live television. He and his men had no message, political or otherwise. They were simply evil, bloodthirsty men who insanely believed murdering Nate on live television would demonstrate to the world the reach of their power. As the entire staff was now either hiding or lying on the ground, one of the shooters began slowly walking closer to Nate. With his gun aimed directly at his forehead, he was now in full view of the camera as Rob, Rick, Kim, and hundreds of thousands of viewers watched helplessly.

Fadi was pleased as he watched the shocking event unfold on live television. He also had a point of view angle transmitted via miniature video cameras the men had strapped to their foreheads. Just as Fadi was about to give the kill order, a deep, booming voice came over the loudspeakers in the studio that were used to communicate between the control room and the anchors when they were off the air. "Mr. Fadi, I warn you to order your men to stand down immediately." The candidates froze as the voice commanded.

Rob looked at his dad and Kim in disbelief. "Oh my God. That's the voice! That's the same person who video called us! They somehow hacked into the control room at the station!"

The menacing voice continued, "Mr. Fadi, we know who you are, we know what you have done, we know where your homes and families are. You cannot hide from us, and we will not hesitate to use our information to destroy you. Your men will place their weapons on the floor and lie face down, spread eagle on the floor immediately. A SWAT team and the Dallas Metro Police have already been notified and are one block away. Check that, the SWAT team is now entering the building.

Mr. Fadi, we have extensive evidence on multiple flash drives proving your connection to the murders of Dr. Francis Crick, Dr. Thomas Smythe, and Dr. Fred Ressner. If any harm comes to any of the people you and Argos have been hunting, the information on these drives will be released on multiple social platforms around the world. Your life as you know it will cease to exist.

The immense rage and anger Fadi was feeling was only surpassed by his confusion and panic. He needed to know who these people were. His mind was already planning on retaliation.

As quickly as the call came into the station, all communications ended, and the live feed was finally cut as the SWAT team stormed the studio and secured the building. Nate would never be able to air the segment, but he was alive. As soon as his heart rate was under control and the police had taken the men out of the station, he called Rob. On the verge of tears, Nate was relieved to hear his friend's voice. "Rob, thank God you're OK. I thought I was a dead man."

"Yeah, I thought you were too. We were watching it on live television up in Denver!" said Rob.

They couldn't talk any longer as Nate had to call his parents and then tell his story to the Dallas police. After hanging up, Rob, his dad, and Kim got back in the truck for the 45-minute drive to her home in Boulder.

Fritz had survived for 3 days on hamburgers, bacon, and waffles. After finally giving him some real dog food, Kim poured her guests three doubles of Stranahan's bourbon on ice while Rick started a fire. It was late May, so evenings in the Rockies could be chilly. They all relaxed by the fire in Kim's living room and talked about the events of the last 3 days. Getting everything out and off their chests was a relief, but when Kim began crying again talking about Fred, Rick moved closer to console her. They were still talking when Rob's cell phone rang again with another video request from an unknown caller and said, "Shit. Here we go again, guys." He swiped the accept button, put the call on speaker so everyone could listen, then sat back as the same voice that had called him and then the station spoke.

"Mr. Wiley, we're glad you all made it safely to Mrs. Ressner's. You won't have to worry about Argos ever again. You will be receiving a copy of Nate's segment on a flash drive, along with information on other oil field replenishments if you choose to continue with the work. We hope that you do."

"But wait, who are you?"

"I cannot divulge that information. But Mrs. Ressner, please know that Fred was an awesome mentor and an incredible teacher. He will be greatly missed." With that, the conversation ended, leaving Kim with a strange feeling.

"What is it, Kim? Are you OK?"

"Yes, I'm fine, Rick. It's just that… well, the caller said Fred was a great mentor. The only people Fred ever mentored were his three interns at school. Oh my God! The last thing Fred said to me before he died was Henry!"

The fire began to dwindle, and the bourbon mixed with mental and physical exhaustion had sat in. They all said their good nights to each other and turned in for the night.

The next morning the golden yellow sun had been up for nearly 3 hours on a crisp morning before Kim finally rolled out of bed. She had been asleep for over 10 hours and got the rest she badly needed. Rob and Rick had already made themselves at home in the kitchen and surprised Kim with a high-fat, high-carb, high-salt breakfast. They didn't know that she was really a granola and oat milk type. She was nonetheless thrilled to share the pancakes and bacon they had made her. It was the first time anyone had cooked her breakfast since she was still in high school and living with her parents. After breakfast, Kim drove them to the Denver Airport, where the three shared an emotional goodbye before she drove back home to Boulder.

After making it through TSA screening and walking through the terminal to their gate, they waited for the flight that would take them back home to Texas. They sat waiting for the next 45 minutes and talked about the ranch, Gina, Rob's job, and their own relationship. Surprisingly to both of them, it wasn't nearly as awkward as they thought it would be.

After running out of conversation, they began watching the people and the planes come and go and joked about which plane they were going to buy when they discovered their next major oil reserve. When Rick saw the Citation X roll by the large picture window overlooking the runway, he smiled and said to Rob, "That's it, son. That's the one I'm gonna buy for you." They both laughed as the gate attendant announced that boarding had begun for their flight home. They would soon be back home in Midland to put their lives back together. They were both anxious to go home and try to make up for so many years they had lost. As they both grabbed their backpacks and began walking down the boarding bridge, neither of them saw who was about to exit from the Citation X.

About the Author

Blood of the Earth author Maury Stoner draws upon his 35-year career in industrial chemicals and environmental awareness to create an incredibly insightful work of fact-based fiction. Growing up in Southern Indiana and later spending time in Texas, these settings are woven together to create a wonderfully written novel. Maury lives in the greater Nashville, Tennessee, with his wife, Heidi.

Made in the USA
Columbia, SC
30 July 2023

21062602R00161